THE DEMON KING'S
TEACHER

EverEri

CONTENT WARNING

The content in this book may not be suitable for everyone. Please beware that this book contains the following:

Explicit sex scenes

Anal

Bondage

Mild SA (Not from MMC)

Violence.

DEDICATION

To every bright light in the world, don't let the darkness diminish
your worth.

For my dearest L.C. Thank you for always being a source of sunshine in my life. You have been by my side, even in the darkest of times, and I don't know where I'd be without you.

Chapter 1

My footsteps sounded like thunder with each step I took towards the demon king's office. Never once in my two decades at Ethlow, the demon king's estate, had I been called to the king's office. My goal was to be the perfect resident. Punctuality was paramount for me when teaching the children. I helped other residents when they fell sick or were overwhelmed. I was kind to everyone. I made every effort to stay out of trouble.

I went over every little thing I had done the past week that could have warranted a scolding from the king. I took an extra muffin from the kitchen, but there wasn't a rule for how much we were allowed to eat—at least that I was aware of. Other than that, I couldn't think of anything.

I swallowed as I reached the black staircase with the gold railing. In twenty years, I had never been to that area. For a long time, the demon king's wing of the estate was forbidden to enter, unless a resident's job required them to clean in that area. That had changed shortly after the newest resident, Nyri, had arrived back in spring—a story I ached to hear.

Each step up the once forbidden staircase made my lungs ache. Anxiety over what was to come was part of it. The other part was my body. Years of living at Ethlow had added weight to my hips—not that I had ever really been small. I had struggled with staying slender for most of my life. It made me stand out among the other pixies in my flock. Most pixies were slender, adding the petite image many had of them. It only added to me feeling as if there was something wrong with me.

If I had used my wings instead of climbing the stairs, my lungs would've been fine, but I hadn't flown since the day my flock had been murdered. There wasn't anything wrong with my wings—at least nothing that Satella, the healer, had figured out. But whenever I tried to fly, it was as if there was a disconnect between my brain and my body. I stopped trying years ago after a nasty fall that ended in a sprained ankle.

When I reached the large black doors of the demon king's office, there was a sharp pain in my side. I pressed my hand against my ribs, wanting to take a moment to catch my breath. I studied the gold inlets in the door, tracing the intricate patterns with my eyes.

The door opened, making me yelp. In front of me stood Master Viridian. He was King Zathrian's right-hand demon, and he was the one truly responsible for keeping Ethlow running smoothly. His teal eyes flared with irritation, and his bat-winged horns fluttered.

"How long were you planning on standing outside?" His dry tone made me flinch. The master of the house had never been rude to me per se, but his intense glare made me nervous. It was as if he was waiting for me to make a mistake.

I cleared my throat. "I was about to knock."

The flat stare he gave me said he didn't believe me. Master Viridian stepped to the side and motioned for me to enter. I swallowed hard as I moved past him, barely able to squeeze through the space he allowed. King Zathrian sat in a large throne-like chair, barely containing his massive size. His leathery wings were folded behind him, and his golden eyes gleamed. The moment he saw me, his face split into a wide grin, making him look more innocent than a demon ever should have.

"Elcy, it's good to see you. Please sit." King Zathrian motioned towards the chair across the desk. I had never had a proper conversation with the king, which only made me more nervous. During the majority of the time I had spent at Ethlow, it had been forbidden to interact with the demon king. For nearly two decades, he had been nothing more than an illusive figure.

As I sat, the master of the house stood behind the king. The demon looked like a bodyguard, ready to use his shadows to kill anyone who threatened the king.

I shifted in the chair, unable to sit still as I waited for the scolding to come. "Hello, your majesty."

"Please call me Zathrian." The king gave a reassuring smile, but it didn't make me feel any better. It was strange to drop the title of authority figures.

"Sire, you must stop telling everyone to address you informally. It'll give the wrong impression." Master Viridian had a perfect posture with his gloved hands tucked behind his back.

The king simply laughed. "Don't mind him." He leaned in a little and whispered, "That's why he doesn't have any friends."

Master Viridian held still, as if he hadn't heard the king, but it was a small room and the king wasn't good at whispering.

I bit back a smile, afraid of accidentally insulting the master of the house. Even though the king was comfortable enough to tease the demon, I didn't dare join in.

"If you don't mind, why am I here? If it's about that muffin, I presumed it wouldn't be of much significance, but I'd be happy to help Aukina cook another batch." I had been sure no one had seen me snatch it, but that was more so because I didn't want anyone to see me take the snack. Others had a tendency to assume my weight was because I overindulged in food. Perhaps it was true to a certain extent, but it was only one reason I looked the way I did.

King Zathrian let out a loud guffaw, making my body tense. It was as if nothing in the world had ever bothered the demon king, but I knew that wasn't true. It wasn't long ago that rumors of his beloved being poisoned had floated around the estate. I was sure he had been a mess during the whole thing. If someone I loved had been on their deathbed, I wouldn't have been able to function.

"No, this is about a much more serious matter. You may eat as much food as your heart desires." King Zathrian clasped his hands together and leaned forward.

The air shifted, growing thicker with each breath. I couldn't think of anything else I had done wrong, but the serious expression on the king's face was more than I could handle.

"Sire, you're making the pixie panic. She thinks she broke a rule." Master Viridian's eyes danced. He looked like the type that liked to see others squirm.

King Zathrian's eyes widened. "No, no. It's nothing like that. I have called you here because I need your assistance with something extremely important."

My shoulders relaxed, but only a little. "You need my assistance?" I couldn't think what the king of Kinzlea could possibly want from me. Everyone at Ethlow had their role. It was a requirement for staying at the demon king's estate for free. I was the teacher, responsible for a handful of children that ended up with nowhere else to go. I taught them a range of subjects, including manners, history, reading, writing, and any other topic that came up. But it wasn't as if the knowledge I had was anything special.

"I have received information about an ancient artifact I've been searching for. We finally have a location, so I hired a ship captain to help me retrieve it. I'm putting together a team to go with him, and I want you to join."

I was more confused after learning the reason I was called to the king's office. Stealing a muffin made more sense than this. "What kind of help could I possibly be on a quest to retrieve an artifact?" There was a time I flew wild through the forest, stayed up late into the night to watch the stars, and painted the sky with pixie dust. I had dreamed of life and adventures outside of my old life, but that had been a long time ago. Life had not been kind to me, and somewhere along the line, I had stopped dreaming.

"You are a pixie, and we need a pixie's magic," Master Viridian said.

His explanation did little to help. "And why do you need a pixie?"

"From what I had been told, the only way to retrieve the artifact is with the magic of a pixie, an elf, and a fae. I normally wouldn't ask such a thing of you, but pixies don't reside in Kinzlea. In fact, you are the only pixie I know of in my kingdom. I asked Queen Xantya of Lyranta for assistance, but she denied my request. You are our last hope." King Zathrian pinched his lips together, the weight of things far heavier than I understood on his shoulders.

Lyranta had been the kingdom I once called my home, but the demon queen had been nowhere in sight when everything I had known and loved was taken from me. Master Viridian was the one who saved me and brought me to Ethlow.

I took a slow breath, trying to sort through my thoughts and push past the painful memories getting dragged to the surface.

"And what would this quest entail?" I asked. The haunted look in King Zathrian's eyes was almost enough to make me agree to his request without question, but the thought of leaving Ethlow grounded me.

"You would travel with Captain Weyland through the Calamity Sea to an island far off Mithcourt, likely with a few others from Ethlow to assist and protect you. The captain would guide you the entire way and ensure your safe travels. Once you retrieve the artifact, you would return to Ethlow."

I took a slow breath. I had always loved the idea of the sea, but my pixie flock used to live in the forest surrounding Queen Xantya's castle. It was far from the ocean, and we had never left the forest, despite all the times I had begged Matron Felca to explore more of the world. She had claimed that the forest kept us protected.

"Can I think about it?" I wanted to help out the king, but Ethlow had become my home and my safe place. The thought of leaving scared me.

"Take your time," King Zathrian said.

"But not too much time," Master Viridian added.

As I left, I was unsure of what my actual deadline was. I slipped out of King Zathrian's office, lost in thought. I stared at the floor as I walked, so I didn't see the male in front of me. I ran into him, my shoulder hitting a surprisingly hard surface. I stepped back, barely able to catch myself.

I scanned the body in front of me from floor to ceiling. Worn leather boots covered his feet with black pants tucked into the shoes. The pants were loose until they hit his thighs where the material couldn't hide his thick, muscular legs. A white shirt was tucked into his belt, and a long leather jacket covered his torso. I was met with two different eye colors, one silver and one nearly black, matching the silver stripe in his long black hair. His leather hat shadowed his face, nearly hiding the two horns that emerged from his forehead.

"I'm so sorry. I didn't see you there." I blinked at the stranger, the smell of salt and cedarwood caressing my nose. I had never seen the male before. His commanding aura was too prominent to forget.

"You should watch where you're going. You never know who'll bite." He clicked his teeth together, revealing two sets of canines.

My heart skipped a beat, entranced by the domineering nature of the male in front of me. He wasn't human. That much was clear by the magic that oozed off of him. It wasn't until he pushed past me that I understood what he was.

He was a demon.

Chapter 2

The mess hall buzzed with a new wave of rumors. I sat at a table alone, listening to the different stories being told. The juiciest gossip always came from the mess hall. Everyone at the estate liked to chatter about everyone else's business, and it had become one of my favorite pastimes. Today, I listened for a different reason.

"Did you hear that the dreaded pirate Captain Weyland is visiting the demon king?" an elf whispered in a volume that resembled nothing of a whisper.

"I heard he is here to collect a new crew."

"What happened to his old one?"

"They say he ate them when they were stranded on an island. Merchants traveling by found him, but there was nothing left of the others from the ship, except the bones he had picked clean."

"I heard he made a crown out of the bones of his crew."

"No, you're wrong. They were the bones of a dragon."

"He couldn't defeat a dragon."

"The dreaded demon pirate Captain Weyland could!"

I tapped the table next to my untouched plate of food. King Zathrian hadn't mentioned the male I was supposed to travel with being a demon. Or a pirate. But that was the one detail every single rumor had in common. Since it was the common factor, there was no doubt it was true. The rest of the rumors were up in the air, and it was impossible for me to tell which gruesome adventure was a fairy tale and which was real. If any of them were real, I knew I couldn't agree to King Zathrian's request.

But the plea in his eyes had tugged at my heart. I ran my fingers through my blonde hair, conflicted about what to do. I had spent the last twenty years wasting my life away, and this was a chance to get away and do something real, but I couldn't travel with a demon pirate. I wanted to have an adventure. I didn't want my bones turned into a crown.

"I can't believe you made me participate in the training class." The familiar voice of the estate's healer, Satella, hit my ears. She walked with her group of friends: Nyri, Aukina, and Tareen. I had seen them hanging out together more and more recently. It'd be a lie to say I wasn't jealous. I was friends with a lot of residents, but I didn't hang out with them at the same caliber as that group of friends.

Nyri caught me staring at them, and her eyes widened. I glanced away, trying to stay calm, but my face grew heated. As a pixie, it was nearly impossible to hide emotions. My skin reacted to whatever feeling bloomed in my chest, and my skin tinged pink with embarrassment.

"Elcy, right?" Nyri approached me, the others following close behind her.

I looked up and smiled. It was easy to smile, even if I felt embarrassed. "That's me."

I had seen the human around the estate, but we had never had a proper conversation before. I knew plenty about her from rumors, so I was sure half of my information was false. What I did know was that she was Satella's friend, and Satella had a beautiful soul. She was one of the residents who came to me to get her nails done, and I always enjoyed talking to her. If she liked Nyri and the others, I knew I'd like them, too.

"Why are you eating alone?" Nyri asked, tilting her head to the side. "Are you waiting for someone?"

I looked around, suddenly self-conscious about sitting by myself. It rarely bothered me, since I enjoyed listening to other conversations, especially with my pixie hearing, but as the group of friends stood in front of me, I didn't want to say the truth.

I pushed a piece of my hair out of my face. "Not tonight."

Nyri pinched her lips together. "You should join us next time you don't have someone to sit with."

I looked at the others, waiting for them to reject the idea, but no one said anything. "That sounds fun." It felt like being invited into the popular group. I didn't know if others saw them that way, but Nyri was the demon king's chosen mate. She was practically royalty.

"Great!" Nyri looked back at the others. "You guys go on ahead."

Satella ignored Nyri, flashing her nails at me. Two of them were broken, which explained the vampire's twisted expression. "They made me attend the training class today, and look what happened. Do you have time to fix my nails soon?"

"I always have time for you." Satella was my best customer at the estate. Others came and went as they wanted their nails done, but Satella stuck to a regular schedule, rarely letting her nails grow out before she asked me to touch them up.

"You're the best." She hugged me and kissed my cheek before departing with everyone except Nyri. Warmth bloomed in my chest from the compliment.

Nyri slid into the seat across from me. "Have you ever been to the greenhouse?" Her eyes were wide with innocence, nothing like how I expected a demon king's lover to be.

I shook my head. "Not yet. I've been meaning to take the children there for a lesson, but I haven't planned it."

"Are you busy now?"

"No."

Nyri beamed. "Now you are."

I followed Nyri through the greenhouse. The repairs to the once broken building were mesmerizing. Last I saw the place, plants had taken over the broken walls, and debris had covered the floor. It resembled nothing of the desolate building it had once been. Plants sat in organized rows with neatly trimmed leaves. The floors were clean, and the glass walls were clear and polished. If Nyri hadn't told me a little about how the greenhouse came to be repaired, I wouldn't have realized it was the same building.

"Without this place, I don't know if Zath and I would have gotten together." There was a twinkle in her eye as she spoke. She loved talking about her origin story with the demon king.

"You're brave for approaching King Zathrian in the first place," I said. Demons made me nervous, which felt ridiculous. I lived under the demon king's protection. Ethlow was the safest place in all of Kinzlea because of the king's generosity. I knew not all demons were bad, but Matron Felca had drilled it into my head that demons were not to be trusted. After eight decades of listening to that belief, it had taken time to unlearn the bias.

"It wasn't as hard as I would have thought." Nyri ran her fingers over a blue vine, and the plant perked up in response to her. Magic caressed the air, and it felt like a warm hug. I had heard rumors about her having magic, but that was the first time I had witnessed it. "Zath was kind to me from the beginning. Kinder than my family had been to me. It was scarier to stay away from him than to give him a chance."

I smiled, thinking back on the meeting with the king. He had been all smiles and laughter. It was the master of the house that made me nervous. "He seems like a good male."

"The best." The smile on Nyri's face only brightened. She continued walking, checking on various plants. I was content moving in silence, but it wasn't long before Nyri spoke. "I have to admit, I had an alternative reason for asking you to come to the greenhouse with me."

"Oh?" The human didn't seem like the type to have an underlying agenda for anything.

"You looked stressed sitting at that table alone. I wanted to make sure you were okay." Nyri stopped, turning to face me. She scanned my face, as if she could see right through the facade I had donned for our interaction.

"I'm fine." I didn't know Nyri well enough to dump my problems onto her. Besides, I was good at dealing with my struggles on my own.

"And that is code for you're not fine, but you don't want to be a burden." Nyri lifted her brows expectantly. "So spill."

My mouth fell open. I didn't understand how she could see right through me. "I don't want to encumber you. I'm sure there is a lot you are dealing with." If the rumors were true, it hadn't been that long since she had come back from the brink of death.

Nyri linked her arm with mine and led me deeper into the greenhouse. "I have the energy to spare for you, otherwise I wouldn't have asked."

I took a deep breath, trying to sort my feelings. Under different circumstances, I would have brushed the offer away, but I needed to bounce my thoughts off someone else.

"I was called into King Zathrian's office today." I waited for her reaction. Since she shared a bed with the king, I had expected her to know this information, but her brows furrowed. I continued on, assuming she hadn't heard about what was happening. "He said he needed my help to retrieve some artifact, but I don't know what to do. I don't know if I could handle an adventure like that."

Nyri's face pinched together. "I don't know what Zath asked of you exactly, but I know he doesn't ask for favors lightly. If he reached out to you, he likely didn't have any other options."

"That's what he said." I dropped my arms. "But I think he asked the wrong person. I can't venture out with a pirate demon to retrieve a lost artifact. That is something heroes do. Not pixies who couldn't save her flock."

Nyri took both of my hands. "You can be the hero in your own story, if that's what you want. I've seen the way you're always helping others."

Nyri didn't know me, but as she stared at me with complete conviction, it made me want to believe her.

"What if you're wrong?"

"I'm not." Her soft smile held unwavering confidence. "But Zath would never force you to do something you don't want to."

"Even if I'm his last resort?" I asked.

Nyri squeezed my hands. "Not if you don't want to. He's not that kind of demon."

I nodded, feeling a little more sure of my decision, but that thought scared me. There was a difference between helping out other residents and leaving the estate with a pirate to retrieve some ancient artifact. I was insane for considering the demon king's request.

Chapter 3

The communal bath house was empty, to my relief. I didn't use the room often, since my room had running water. Whenever I wanted to take a proper bath, I had no choice but to use the communal one. The bath in my room was too small to fit my wings and thick thighs comfortably. Most days, I was fine letting the water pour over my head to get clean.

But with the weight of the king's request on my shoulders, I needed the steam from a hot bath to flush away my thoughts and worries. I undressed as the water filled the copper tub. I dipped my toes in first, hissing at the burn of the water. It was a little too hot, but it was exactly what I needed. I slid in slowly, my skin turning red from the temperature threatening to boil me alive. My wings curled around me as I leaned back.

I breathed in the steam, letting it relax my muscles, but the tension in my shoulders refused to release. After what Nyri had said, I wanted to help the king, but there was so much unknown to his proposal. I needed to ask him for details—especially about the captain I was supposed to travel with. I wanted to help King Zathrian after he allowed me to stay at his estate when I had nowhere else to go, but this differed from helping out in the kitchen when someone was sick. This favor involved leaving Ethlow.

When I first arrived, I had told myself constantly that I was going to leave one day, but then I settled into a comfortable routine. Slowly, the idea of leaving became less appealing until I decided it was better to stay. It was safe in the demon king's estate, which meant I'd stay alive. It had been over a decade since I had thought about starting over somewhere new.

My energy buzzed the more I thought about life outside of Ethlow. It wasn't like King Zathrian was asking me to leave permanently. Just go on some grand adventure with a demon pirate to collect an ancient artifact across the seas. It was a ridiculous thought when I put it that way.

I blew bubbles as I let out a long breath. Who was I kidding? I wasn't the adventuring type. Not anymore. Nyri was being too nice before. Or she knew how important the ask was for the demon she loved.

I was stuck in a loop of thoughts, and my wings vibrated, releasing pixie dust into the tub. The magic wrapped around the water, lifting water bubbles into the air. Gold dust swirled around the water, making the room glitter from the low light. I giggled as balls of water floated, hovering over the bath. I poked one with my finger, and the water burst, raining back down. Another giggle spilled out of my mouth, taking delight in the small act.

"You're easily impressed, aren't you?" The deep voice snapped me out of the moment.

I tensed, covering my bare chest with my hands. I glanced over my shoulder, and my heart rate went wild as I saw the demon pirate leaning against the wall of the bathhouse. His jacket was missing, and his white shirt was especially low cut, showing off the muscles beneath.

"What are you doing here?" I squeaked. I hated feeling exposed, especially in front of a stranger. My body wasn't the shape others usually fawned over, so I preferred hiding it from the world.

His hat shadowed his eyes, making it nearly impossible to read his face. "This is the community bath, is it not?" He wasn't wrong, but that didn't lessen my embarrassment.

I grabbed my towel and wrapped it around me as I stood. "That doesn't give you a right to peep on unsuspecting women like a creep."

Captain Weylan stroked his chin, taking his time to respond. "I'm too attractive to be considered a creep."

My eyes widened in disbelief. Did he really just say that? I stormed up to him, holding my towel as tightly around me as possible. With my plush waist, the towel didn't close around my body entirely, leaving a slit open on my leg, but my boiling blood made it easy to forget about that.

"I don't care how attractive you are. You can't watch people in the bath." I huffed, puffing my chest out.

Captain Weyland took two fingers and lifted my chin, his mismatched eyes meeting mine. "Maybe I am here to take a bath, and you happened to be here."

The steam I had a moment ago disappeared, my voice with it. "Are you here to take a bath?"

"Why? Do you want to watch?" His subtle wink made me grow flustered.

"No," I snapped. I pushed his hand away, but he only smirked.

"It's going to be fun having you on my deck."

"Excuse me?" I choked out.

"I hear you're going to join me on my ship." He took a step back, leaning against the wall. The movement tipped his hat forward, hiding his face from me.

"I haven't decided yet." I stepped back, slowly becoming more aware of my lack of clothes. I couldn't remember the last time I had spoken to anyone with this little coverage on my body.

He huffed a laugh. "Yes, you have."

"No, I haven't. Don't act like you know me." I stomped my foot as I looked at the pirate.

Captain Weyland pushed off the wall and stalked forward. I held my ground, even as he hovered over me. His height made me feel tiny. "You faced something tragic. Let me guess. Your childhood pet died unexpectedly? Or maybe you were separated from your family in a terrible way? Yes. That's the one." He paused, giving me a chance to confirm, but I pressed my lips together. "Ever since, you've been hiding away in the demon king's estate. For a while, you told yourself you would return to the real world, but fear stopped you. You've grown complacent in your life."

He reached down to cup my cheek. "But there's a piece of you missing. You are craving adventure, and I'm the one who can give that to you. That's how I know you'll end up taking a ride on my deck."

The air in the room felt strangely thin. "I'm not interested in your deck."

"We'll see about that." Captain Weyland winked and let go of me. "Now, if you don't mind, I'm going to take a bath." He walked towards the tub and took off his hat, revealing a pair of short horns. He stripped his shirt next. Tattoos of chains covered his muscular back, starting from his spine between his shoulder blades before spreading out in four directions, two that wrapped around his arms and two that crossed over his torso. He reached for his pants next, pulling his belt away slowly.

I found myself mesmerized by his movements. My eyes traced the dark curves and lines inked into his skin. My fingers twitched as I imagined tracing those lines.

Captain Weyland glanced over his shoulder. "Are you planning on watching the entire time?"

His words yanked me out of my trance. I rushed to grab my stuff and ran out of the bathhouse, the low chuckle of the demon following after.

Chapter 4

"**E**lcy? You good?" Satella waved her hands in front of me, pulling me out of my thoughts. I had been thinking about my interaction with Captain Weyland in the communal baths, but I wasn't about to tell her that.

"Sorry. I spaced out for a moment." I dipped my brush in black paint mixed with pixie dust and stroked it over her nails. I did nails for several of the residents at Ethlow, and my list of customers had been growing as of late. Recently, the librarian had also become a regular, making it difficult to find time to do everyone's nails and teach, while aiding others in the estate. There were many days I felt stretched thin, but I found it difficult to say no when others asked me for a favor.

"I noticed." Satella let out a low chuckle. "Let me guess, you are thinking about Captain Weyland and the favor Zathrian asked of you."

"How do you know about that?" It was as if she had read my mind, but vampires didn't have the power to do that—as far as I knew.

"You should know that nothing stays secret in the estate. Also, Nyri doesn't know how to keep a secret to save her life." Satella shifted her hands, making it easier to paint her nails. It had become a routine for us, since we had done it hundreds of times over the past two decades.

I hadn't planned on talking to anyone else about my dilemma. Nyri had listened, so I didn't need to bother Satella with it, too. "I don't know what to do. The thought of going back into the real world is terrifying. I'm too old for that, but if the king needs my help, I don't want to say no."

Satella lifted her brows. "How old are you, exactly?"

"I'm turning one hundred a week after the winter solstice."

"You're a baby. I'm centuries older than you, and pixies live to what? Six, seven hundred years?"

"Sometimes eight," I corrected. When I thought about my life span, I knew the healer was right.

"Then you should live your life while you're young. Don't let yourself get stuck here."

"Do you ever plan on leaving?" It wasn't common for residents to leave the estate after arriving. In the twenty years I had been at Ethlow, more residents had died than left of their own accord.

Satella shrugged. "I'm happy here, and I'm too old for adventure. But you are too bright to get stuck in the darkness of this place. The world needs your kindness."

I finished the vampire's last nail and quickly packed my supplies. "Thank you for listening to me."

Satella wiggled her fingers, smiling at the design. "Anytime. You should hurry before you're late. Those children get wild."

I glanced outside, realizing she was right. I was already running late to the classroom.

As I opened the door, the sound of clinking metal filled my ears. I froze, familiar with those sounds. They were the same ones that came from the barracks when the guardsmen were training. They did not belong in the classroom.

As I rushed inside, two of the children jumped from desk to desk, swinging swords wildly. Thalanil and Galia were only fourteen and twelve, and as far as I knew, they had no weapon training.

"I'm going to cut out yer tongue!" Galia jumped closer to Thalanil, using her harpy wings to help her float to the next desk.

"Not before I steal your booty!" Thalanil jumped away. He landed on the edge of a desk, making the entire thing wobble. His arms flailed as he fell backwards. He barely managed to land on his feet, his werewolf senses kicking in.

"What is going on here?" I demanded, making both children freeze.

"That's what I want to know." The deep voice sent a chill down my spine. The energy in the room darkened as shadows crawled around the floor. I didn't have to turn around to know the master of the house stood behind me.

I swallowed hard, spinning slowly to meet the gaze of the shadow demon. "Master Viridian. What are you doing here?"

His face was like a statue, impossible to read. "I came to discuss something with you, Miss Elcy." His eyes slid to the children behind me. Galia froze on top of the desk with her arm holding the sword above her head. "Is this how you run your classroom?"

My chest tightened at the accusation. "No, it's usually not this chaotic. I swear." My words seemed to do nothing to change the opinion of the demon. Why did Master Viridian have to show up the one day I was running late and the children were unusually out of hand?

"I see." He shifted his attention to Galia and Thalanil. "Children your age should not be playing with weapons as if they are toys." He snapped his fingers, and shadows swallowed the pair of swords, leaving the two empty-handed. "If I catch you playing with dangerous tools again, you'll face serious consequences. Do you understand?" When neither child answered, he repeated. "Do you *understand*?"

"Yes, Master Viridian," Galia and Thalanil said at the same time.

The muscle in Master Viridian's jaw feathered. He didn't look satisfied, but I wasn't sure if the demon was capable of that feeling. "Now get off the desk and clean up this mess while I speak to your teacher."

Galia jumped to the ground, using her wings to make her glide gently to her feet. She offered her hand to Thalanil, and neither of them dared to argue with the master of the house.

"Come," Master Viridian snapped at me. He turned and stepped into the hallway.

I followed, also knowing better than to talk back to the demon. I gave Thalanil and Galia a warning look before stepping outside. The last thing I needed was for more chaos to erupt while the master of the house was visiting.

"I plan to have a thorough talk with them," I said the second the door shut. I had been perfectly fine keeping to myself. It was better than the attention that swarmed me since the demon king requested my help.

Master Viridian ignored my statement, no longer interested in that conversation. "Have you decided whether or not you will assist the sire with the quest?"

"Not yet. It's a big decision, and I want to help, but I'm just unsure if I'm suited for something like that." I was leaning towards accepting, but there was an uncertainty holding me back.

"I thought that might be the case." Master Viridian adjusted his glove. "Meet me in the grand hall at sunset. There is something you need to see that will help you decide."

"What is it?" I asked.

"You will see. Do not be late." Master Viridian stepped back into the shadows, disappearing before I could respond.

The moment he was gone, it was easier to breathe. I wanted to take a moment before dealing with the children, but after what I had witnessed, I didn't want to leave them alone for a moment longer. When I came back inside, the room looked immaculate. They had cleaned and organized it in the short time I had been gone. Master Viridian had a way of striking fear into the hearts of residents and getting results I knew I never could.

When they saw me, Thalanil and Galia stopped cleaning, their heads falling in shame.

"You two got me in trouble with Master Viridian," I said, shaking my head. If this had happened a few days ago, it wouldn't have been an issue. The timing couldn't have been worse.

"We didn't mean to," Thalanil said. He looked up before flicking his hair out of his face. He had grown so much since he arrived at the estate. It wouldn't be long before he grew up into a young man.

"What in the great world were you two doing with weapons? You could have seriously gotten hurt." I easily slipped into my teacher's voice as I scolded them.

"We wanted to be cool like the infamous Captain Weyland," Galia said. "I heard he faced three sea monsters and killed them with his bare hands."

"I heard he has destroyed pirate ships without getting a scratch on him!" Thalanil's face perked up.

Captain Weyland wasn't without scars. I knew that for a fact, but that wasn't something I was about to divulge to children. "You can't believe any rumor you hear about others."

"But have you seen him?" Galia asked. "You can tell he's powerful from across the room. I want to be a pirate when I grow up and leave this place."

"Being a pirate isn't some glamorous thing." I didn't like the idea of Galia growing up only to run into a life of thievery. There were so many other things someone like her could do.

"But pirates live a life free from rules!" Thalanil said. "No one to tell them what to do or what to read. They get to fight others and have really cool adventures."

"They also die at sea." I hoped to strike fear into the children's hearts to discourage them from an immoral life, but it did no good.

"Yeah, but a life on the seas is worth it. Just think about all the things you'll get to see." Galia placed her hands on her hips.

I could see where the conversation was going, and I didn't want to dwell on the pirate captain. "Okay, that's enough about pirates. Everyone find your seats and get ready for our first lesson: the dangers of wielding weapons you have no training in." I gave Thalanil and Galia pointed looks. It wasn't a lesson I had thought I would teach today, but the last thing I needed was any injuries because of the excitement Captain Weyland's visit stirred up at Ethlow.

Chapter 5

I glanced outside, waiting for the sun to set. Master Viridian had been very clear about not being late, but sunset was a wide range of time. Did he mean when the sky shifted colors because of the angle of the sun or when the sun had fully sunk below the horizon? I arrived early just to be safe. I didn't need more negative attention from the master of the house.

The moment the mountains covered the sun, shadows swirled into the room. Master Viridian stepped out of them, looking as pristine as ever. He nodded in greeting when he saw me.

"You don't have a coat."

I looked at my clothing, already knowing that. Winter had crept to the estate, but it was too early for snowfall. "I didn't think I'd need a coat. We're not allowed to go outside at night." If anyone knew the rules set forth for the residents, it was Master Viridian.

"Not tonight. I'm taking you outside Ethlow's protection." Master Viridian's eyes flashed as he stared at me.

It wasn't a joke, which made my throat go dry. One of the first things I was told when I first arrived was to never step foot outside the walls of the estate after dark. The rule was set in place for the safety of the residents. Dangerous creatures lurked outside at night, and the demon king could only protect those inside the walls of the estate. Months ago, I had heard a rumor about Aukina, the head cook, nearly getting killed when she failed to make it inside before dark.

"Is this a punishment for earlier?"

"No." Master Viridian held out his hand. He wasn't going to explain further.

My instincts told me to run. Wherever this demon wanted to take me was dangerous, but there was no choice. Even if I ran, Master Viridian would find me. I swallowed hard as I gripped his white glove. Shadows burst from the demon without warning. The darkness wrapped around me, swallowing me whole. A firm hand held onto mine. It was the only thing that kept me grounded in the whirl of shadows. The darkness was a place many had gotten lost in before. Time and light didn't exist in the world I had been dragged into.

When the world returned, it felt like it was spinning. Master Viridian kept a firm grip on my hand. It was the only thing that stopped me from falling over.

"Take a deep breath. It helps," the demon said.

I did as ordered. It lessened the nausea slightly, but it didn't stop my head from spinning. The demon released my hand before I was ready, but I didn't complain. The master of the house did everything with intent.

"Do you know the real reason residents are forbidden outside Ethlow at night?" Master Viridian clasped his hands behind his back and looked at the world below us.

I followed his gaze, realizing we stood on top of a cliff that overlooked the estate. "Because it's dangerous." As the light continued to fade, unnatural shadows moved between the trees.

"But why is it dangerous? Not all of Kinzlea is threatened at night. Only the area immediately around the demon king." Master Viridian looked at me and waited. He wasn't going to give the answer easily.

I scrunched my nose as I thought about it. He was right. It wasn't dangerous to be outside at night in other parts of the kingdom. Only at Ethlow. I had never thought about the logistics of it before, but it was strange. I didn't understand why, but I thought about the lessons I taught the children in class.

Then it clicked.

I looked up at Master Viridian. He towered over me. As a pixie, I was shorter than many beings. The only ones shorter than me at Ethlow were the gnomes and goblins. "Does it have something to do with King Zathrian being from the underworld?"

Demons originated from the underworld, but the veil between the mortal realm and the underworld wasn't a barrier most could travel through with ease, demons included. Every demon that lived in the mortal realm had either escaped from the underworld during the Great Demon Wars or were born among mortals after. Only the oldest demons could claim they were truly from the underworld.

"You're smarter than I expected," Master Viridian said. He stepped forward, shifting his attention back to the forest below. "What many don't know is that the Great Demon War occurred when demons decided they no longer wanted to live in the underworld—don't ask why, because I won't tell you. Their unrest grew so great that they searched for ways to cross into the mortal realm permanently. When they found a way, they ripped open the veil between two worlds, not caring about the ramifications to the mortal realm."

"The five most powerful demons that crossed into the mortal realm found a way to repair that tear, and they promised to help in exchange for kingdoms. What they didn't know was that over the centuries, the veil grew weak. You see, the ruler of the underworld doesn't like to be betrayed. He wants to take back what belongs to him. It seems he is forcing the veil to break, and the cracks are occurring beneath King Zathrian's feet. Quite literally."

Master Viridian gestured towards the estate. The light from the sun was gone, giving way to twisted shadows. Then it happened. It looked as if the ground had cracked open. A large creature emerged from the darkness beneath. It walked on ten legs, and it had a big, bulky body. With each step, it looked as if its skin was melting off its bones, but the look of the creature wasn't the worst part. The smell hit me, making me gag. It was as if flesh had been rotting in a sewer.

I threw my hands over my mouth, barely breathing to avoid the smell. There had always been talks of the dangers outside the estate, but I had never imagined something like that lingering on the other side of the walls.

Master Viridian turned to me. "King Zathrian has done his best to control it, but it is becoming more difficult for him and the other rulers to keep the veil sealed, which is where you come in. King Zathrian would never force you to help—something I don't agree with—but he needs your help. The artifact he has asked you to retrieve will help keep Ethlow safe, as well as the people you've come to love. You wouldn't want to lose anyone else, would you?"

My hands shook, and my eyes stung from the putrid scent in the air. "Why me?" I barely managed to say. "There has to be someone else who can help."

"You should know better than anyone that the pixie population has dwindled because of hunting. The artifact can't be retrieved with magic from the underworld. Very specific wards were placed on the artifact, and only with a pixie's help can we retrieve it."

My heart sounded like thunder, and I wanted to cry. I hadn't realized Ethlow was in peril. Living at Ethlow was like living in a bubble, safe from the world, but Master Viridian popped that bubble. There was no walking away from this knowledge.

"I'll do it," I whispered.

Master Viridian nodded. "I thought that would be the case once you learned the truth." He held out his hand. "You leave first thing tomorrow morning."

Chapter 6

I stared down at the bowl in front of me, my stomach twisting. The reality of the next couple of weeks settled in, making it difficult to think about eating. In less than a day, I was to leave Ethlow and venture into a world I once knew but was now foreign. There was too much to do before then. I had to tell the children about my absence. I didn't know who was going to take my place as their teacher, either. I couldn't imagine many in the estate being willing to take on the children, even though they were wonderful in their own unique ways. Then there was also the need to pack. I preferred to prepare longer for a trip—not that I had taken more than a stroll outside the walls of Ethlow since arriving twenty years ago.

"Hello." Nyri slid into the seat across from me. She glowed as she smiled, making me feel at ease around her.

"Hello." It was easy to snap back into my cheery state. When others were around, I tried to hide any turmoil poisoning my thoughts.

Nyri didn't have food with her, which told me she wasn't here for a casual conversation. "Zath told me you agreed to help. He is beyond grateful, which I'm sure he'll tell you before you go."

"I'm happy to help the demon king." It was true, which made it easy to say, even if a million worries wracked my mind.

"He finally told me what's going on." Nyri wrinkled her nose, making me wonder what kind of conversations she had had with her lover behind the scenes. "Sometimes it feels like pulling up stubborn roots to get him to talk. I know he wants to protect me, but I'm strong enough to handle the truth." She glanced around the room, checking to see who all was listening to our conversation.

The mess hall was mostly empty, except for the kitchen staff. Everyone else had finished dinner a while ago before turning in for the evening. It left the room empty, but I was sure someone was listening to us. Words spoken within the walls of Ethlow were rarely kept secret. It was as if the shadows heard every word spoken and spread the conversations like rumors.

"It's nice that the demon king cares about you so much." I had only caught glimpses of Nyri and the king together, but the way they smiled at one another made the love they had for one clearer than a spring day.

Nyri's face softened. "I'm incredibly lucky. I know that, but I wish he wouldn't worry so much."

"You almost died at the beginning of fall, didn't you?" The entire estate was affected when Nyri had fallen ill. It was as if a fog of shadows had drowned out any smiles. I had never learned the details of what happened to the demon king's lover, but when she made a full recovery, light returned to the estate.

Nyri pursed her lips. "Yes, which is why I get that he's so protective. I just wished he had told me things had gotten so..." She looked around again. She was fully aware of the fact that we were talking about a dangerous subject in a public place. She lowered her voice, but it didn't stop her from speaking. "Bad. If I had known the estate was in danger... I don't know what I would've done, but I could've been helping him. I knew something was off, but I never would've guessed—" She cut herself off again, searching my eyes.

It wasn't King Zathrian who told me what was happening outside the walls of Ethlow. It was the master of the house, which made me wonder if Nyri knew as much as I did.

"I know," I said. "It feels like the bubble I've been living in popped, which is why I want to do everything in my power to help, as terrifying as it is."

Nyri took my hand. "You have a pure soul. We're lucky to have you here."

I smiled, even as my heart squeezed. Master Viridian gave me a brief rundown of what was to come—only after I had agreed to help. I was to travel with Captain Weyland to Riddler's Cove, where we would board the captain's ship. Then we'd spend weeks traveling to Dragon's Breath Island where we'd retrieve the artifact. If everything went smoothly, I'd be gone for two months total.

The thought unnerved me. Two months was a blip in time, but it was longer than I had ever been out on my own. I spent the first eighty years of my life in my flock and the last twenty at Ethlow.

"It's been a while since I've been in the real world," I said. I didn't know if Nyri could understand what that felt like. She was a human, and a young one at that. I had likely been at Ethlow for nearly as long as she had been alive.

"Maybe it'll do you some good to get out of here," Nyri said to my surprise. She quickly added, "Not that I don't love Ethlow, but it's like what you said. Living here is like living in a bubble, and there is an entire world out there waiting for you to explore it."

I had once thought that way, thinking I would travel to every kingdom and see the mortal realm in its full glory. Before I had gathered the nerve to part with my flock, their blood stained the soil, and I lost my wild desires. "What if I'm not ready to step back into that world?"

Nyri simply smiled. "Then it's a good thing you won't be alone. Zath has asked Aukina and Reamann to go along with you. He thought they'd be helpful."

I glanced at the kitchen where the cook was. She looked like she was busy preparing for lunch, but the way her gills flared showed that the mermaid was listening to the conversation. No conversation was private.

I liked Aukina. I didn't know her well, but I had helped out in the kitchen a few times, and she was always smiling and friendly. And I liked Reamann. He taught a self-defense class weekly, and I joined occasionally. He was patient with everyone, even if they had no fighting skills. It was nice to know I wouldn't be leaving the estate alone.

I waved at Aukina, and her eyes widened. She moved away from the counter that peered into the mess hall, disappearing from sight.

"I'm glad they're coming, but I'm a little surprised they agreed to join." I had seen Aukina's fighting skills in Reamann's class. She was better than some of us, but she was a novice.

"Zath figured Aukina could help if there is any trouble with the sea, and the moment Reamann heard Aukina was being asked to go, he volunteered to join, arguing that he would be the perfect bodyguard for the two of you, but I know the truth. He can't stand the thought of being away from the love of his life for that long." Nyri smiled, twisting her hair around her finger. She loved the idea of love, maybe as much as I did.

"That's cute," I giggled. I pushed down my jealous thoughts, wondering when it'd be my turn to find that kind of connection.

"It's pretty incredible that so many people have found love here," Nyri said. "From what I heard, there was a darkness that held onto the estate before I showed up, but love has bloomed recently. I heard that even Tareen found someone."

My eyes widened. Tareen was the librarian, and she was sweet when I brought the children to look for books. She was also a recluse. I had rarely seen her step outside of the library during my time at Ethlow, and the librarian had been at the demon king's estate for much longer than I had.

"Who?" I asked, unable to hold back my curiosity. I loved hearing about the ongoings of the estate.

Nyri looked around before leaning forward. "King Jathral."

I gasped, covering my mouth with my hand. King Jathral was one of the five demon rulers of the mortal realms, and he had a dubious reputation. I had seen him in the library with Tareen not that long ago, but she looked at him as if she was ready to kill him. It made it difficult to believe the words Nyri had said, but the young human didn't seem like the type to lie.

"Really?"

Nyri tried to hide her smile, but she failed. "Yeah. Zath told me King Jathral even asked him for advice on how to woo Tareen."

My eyes widened even more. "I never would have guessed that."

"But don't tell anyone," Nyri quickly added. "I think the new couple would get too embarrassed if anyone knew how much they cared for each other."

I nodded, understanding, but I was grateful I was leaving the estate soon. I wasn't sure I would have been able to keep a secret like that for long. It was too big and shocking to keep to myself.

"I would love to know the story of how that happened," I said, shaking my head.

"I'll make you a deal. I'll tell you everything I know about the couple when you get back from your trip, if you promise to tell me about your adventure."

"I can do that," I laughed. "But I don't know how exciting it'll be."

"You are traveling with Captain Weyland, pirate king of the sea. If you don't come back with at least ten stories, one of which must be romantic, I will be disappointed."

I lifted my brows slowly. "I don't think there will be much romance on that ship."

Nyri gave me a look that made me shift in my seat. "I've seen that pirate captain, and he is a delicious piece of cake. And I know you're single. If you are going to have a real adventure, you might as well have some fun with the pirate captain."

I chewed on my lip, thinking back to the communal bath house encounter. His attractiveness was undeniable, but he was too cocky for my taste. I preferred the sweet and caring type. "Captain Weyland isn't my type."

"He's a pirate. He doesn't have to be your type. I'm not saying he's the kind you fall in love with. He's the kind you take to bed and tell stories about later. Although, it would be pretty cute if you two fell in love. Oh, that would be so romantic. A pixie and a pirate brought together on an adventure to save the world." Nyri's eyes glimmered with romantic hope.

I wanted to call her crazy, but I couldn't deny that it would have been a beautiful story. I shook off that thought. Captain Weyland didn't seem like the relationship type, and the idea of falling in love at sea wasn't enough to change my mind.

"Not going to happen." I stood, my food still untouched. "Thanks for talking to me. I feel a little better." There was a lot to do before the morning, but the knot in my stomach didn't feel as heavy.

"Of course. And if you need anything before you leave, I'm here for you." Nyri pulled me into a hug unexpectedly, but when I hugged her back, even more weight fell off my shoulders. I quickly made a mental note to take more time to get to know Nyri when I came back from the trip.

If I came back.

Chapter 7

I was the first to arrive at the front of the estate. A carriage sat outside, and it was the largest one I had ever seen. It would fit six people comfortably, plus our luggage.

"I thought you might be the early morning type." Captain Weyland stepped out of the shadows. He wore his hat and his coat to protect him against the icy winter morning.

"I like being punctual." My luggage weighed down my arms, but I was unsure of where to put it. I had only packed two bags, being careful to pack lightly. I had debated bringing more, since I didn't know what I would face in the real world, but I didn't want to bring more than what I could carry.

My wings fluttered as thoughts of the unknown filled my head. Captain Weyland's gaze shifted to my wings, and his silver eye seemed to brighten at the sight. It wasn't uncommon for others to look at my wings with wonderment. Pixies were the only beings whose magic came from their wings. Many thought fairies and pixies were the same, but fairies got their magic from the earth. We looked similar, but we were different in nearly every way that mattered.

Captain Weyland approached, his footsteps heavy in the early morning light. He took my bags from me, easily lifting them. "Let me take that. We don't need a delicate thing like you accidentally hurting yourself."

"Excuse me?" I put my hands on my hips and glared at the pirate captain. "I'm not delicate."

Captain Weyland tossed my belongings onto the back of the carriage. When he turned back, he looked me up and down. "Pixies are notorious for being delicate, especially their wings. It wouldn't take much to injure those precious wings of yours, and if that happens, you won't have much use on my ship."

I huffed at the accusation. He wasn't exactly wrong. If a pixie's wings accidentally got torn, it stopped the production of pixie dust and sometimes led to death if the tear was severe enough. Without our magic and use of our wings, it made us vulnerable. It didn't mean we were fragile. "I'm not delicate, and I wouldn't be useless without my wings." My stomach churned at that thought. If Captain Weyland needed me to fly to retrieve the artifact, then going on this trip was a mistake. I hadn't thought about that since King Zathrian had said he needed a pixie. If they needed a winged being, there were several others with that capability. What made a pixie unique was her pixie dust.

Captain Weyland looked me up and down, licking his lips. "No, you wouldn't be useless, not with that treasure chest of yours." His eyes lowered from mine.

My face instantly heated at the captain's lude comment. My face turned bright red, and there was no use in trying to hide my emotions.

"You'd have to have the key to touch my treasure, and you can start dreaming about that, since it's never going to happen." Despite Nyri's comments making my mind wander briefly, the last thing I needed was to get involved with the pirate. That was asking for heartbreak.

"What if I have already dreamed about your treasure and how warm it would feel wrapped around me?" A smirk danced across Captain Weyland's face, and any sass I had a moment prior disappeared.

"Weyland, are you torturing your special guest?" Master Viridian stepped out of the shadows, coming to my rescue—something I had never thought I'd say about the demon.

"I'm just having a little fun." Captain Weyland didn't take his eyes off me.

I squirmed beneath his gaze, the intensity of it making me question my resolve. The captain would be no good for me, but it didn't stop my mind from wandering to what ifs.

Master Viridian stepped closer to me. "If you do anything to harm the residents under the protection of King Zathrian, you know we'll have a problem." Shadows danced off the demon's shoulders in warning.

A low chuckle escaped from Captain Weyland's mouth. "You might have the demons on these lands shaking from that little trick, but you forget that I'm the king of the sea. I don't play by the same rules as the rest of you." The pirate flared his own powers, and I had to take a step back, afraid I'd get caught in crossfire.

A booming laugh broke the tension between the two demons. King Zathrian stepped out of the estate with his large hand intertwined with Nyri's. "Now, now, there's no need to fight. I'm sure Captain Weyland will take good care of all our people joining his crew." Despite his laugh, there was an intensity to the king's eyes that was unnerving. It was as if he was telling Captain Weyland that if he did anything to hurt us, he would hurt him.

"I will take care of them as well as any other crew member," Captain Weyland said, but his eyes told a different story. There was something between the three demons that went back years, if not decades, and it made me wonder what it was.

"Don't mind them," Nyri said, letting go of King Zathrian's hand and moving towards me. "I have found that many demons like to remind others who is the most powerful in the room."

"I find that to be a common male feature," I said.

Nyri let out a laugh that didn't match the level of my joke. It brought the attention of the demons to us. Captain Weyland looked at me with a single brow raised, as if he didn't expect me to say something like that. Master Viridian looked no different, and King Zathrian smiled in approval.

I shifted, uncomfortable with so many powerful males looking at me. It had been a while since I had had that kind of attention on me.

"When are we supposed to leave?" I asked to change the subject.

"Just as soon as the rest of your companions arrive," Captain Weyland said.

"We're here! Sorry we're late." Aukina rushed out of the front doors with Reamann in tow. He held all of their bags, which was over twice the amount I had, making me wonder if I was under packed.

"Aukina was triple checking that Wistari was okay to take over the kitchen while she was gone." Reamann rolled his eyes, but Aukina couldn't see the gesture.

"I'm the head of the kitchen. I can't leave without proper preparations." Aukina let out an exasperated sigh.

"Ethlow will be fine without you, Miss Aukina," Master Viridian said. "We functioned before you, and I will ensure the estate continues to function long after you." The demon's icy tone made Aukina flinch. It was a harsh reminder that the estate didn't need any of us to continue on. It was a place for us to take refuge, and while we were there, we did our part. Over time, it had become my home, but a single word from the master of the house or the king, and any of us could lose the life we had built.

"As much fun as this has been, we need to get going," Captain Weyland said. "I have already left my crew waiting for long enough because of an indecisive pixie."

I clamped my lips together, resisting the urge to bite back. I didn't want to bark back at the pirate in front of Master Viridian or King Zathrian. It wasn't logical to sass the captain at all, since he was going to be responsible for my life for the next couple of months, but there was something about the pirate demon that made me want to show my claws—not that pixies had claws.

"Wait!" the front door of the estate opened, and Satella rushed out with disheveled hair. She stopped in front of us, breathing deeply. "I thought I was going to miss you."

"You cut it close, Miss Satella." Master Viridian's tone was dry, but it didn't seem to bother the vampire.

Satella lifted her middle finger at the master of the house, which made me blanch. I would have never treated a powerful demon like him with disrespect, especially not when he could kick me out of the place I had made into my home.

The vampire turned to me. "I have a gift for you." She handed me a small box with a black ribbon tied around it.

"What is it?"

Satella smiled. "Tareen and I have been working on healing salves and potions using the bleeding heart lily. It is the most powerful healing tonic I have ever worked with. I figured it could come in handy on your long journey. I want to make sure you come home safe. Who else will do my nails otherwise?" She flashed her newest set of nails.

"You didn't have to do that." The vampire's gift made my lip wobble.

"I did." She wrapped her arms around me, holding me tightly. In my ear, she whispered, "Don't forget how incredible you are, and get home safely. We need you here, okay?" There was something about the vampire's hug that felt healing. I couldn't remember the last time anyone held me with that much care, and it made tears bubble in my eyes.

"Okay," I said, unable to say anything else without fear of crying. The reality of leaving hit me hard.

Satella hugged Aukina and whispered something to the mermaid while Reamann loaded their bags into the carriage. The vampire wrapped Reamann in a hug next, and his eyes widened, as if he was surprised Satella would ever hug him.

The vampire turned to Captain Weyland last. "I'm entrusting you to take care of my friends. Don't disappoint me, or I will haunt you. I have friends in powerful places."

Satella's audacity shocked me, but Captain Weyland looked amused. "I have no intention of letting harm come to the pixie. She's the key to my success."

"You mean the success of the quest," Master Viridian corrected.

"Yes," Captain Weyland drawled, rubbing his jawline. "The success of the quest is my success, after all." He winked at me, which left me dazed. Why did the captain have to be that attractive?

Chapter 8

I t took five days of nearly nonstop traveling through Kinzlea to reach Riddler's Cove. I had expected to stop for the night to stay at an inn, but Captain Weyland insisted we didn't have time or funds to waste on a nice bed for the night. By the end of the five days, my body ached worse than it ever had. Between sleeping in the carriage and the growing winter chill, it was nearly impossible to sleep properly throughout the night.

When we reached the cove, Captain Weyland was the first out of the carriage, followed by Reamann and Aukina. I took my time, surprised by the pops and aches in my joints. I was young at nearly a century old, but it felt like I was five hundred with the way my body hurt.

As I went to step out of the carriage, Reamann was waiting for me. He held out his hand and helped me down the steps.

"I don't think my body has ever hurt like this, even after hours of grueling training," the orange-haired demon chuckled. He smiled brightly, acting nothing like the other demon we had been traveling with. Reamann was a guardsman at Ethlow, but he was a lesser demon. I didn't know the extent of his strength, but my magic could feel the magic others held, and Reamann hardly had any—at least when he was in his human form.

On the first night in the carriage, Reamann had shifted into his demon form, scaring me with the sudden transformation. He explained that he didn't have control over his form like the demon king, since Reamann was only half demon.

"I can't wait for a good night's sleep," I said. I stretched my hands, groaning at the strain in my muscles.

"Don't expect feather beds and luxury on the ship," Captain Weyland said, clearly listening to our conversation. He stood in front of the carriage, looking at the bay. A large ship sat in the center of the water. The sails were all black except for a white stripe running down at an uneven diagonal. A flag with chains in the shape of an X flew high above. Small specks ran around the ship, the shouting of the crew faint from where we stood.

I walked past the captain. My focus wasn't on the ship that would carry us to our next destination. It was on the sea beyond. It stretched on for as far as I could see until it disappeared into the horizon. The sinking sun reflected off the water in pink and orange hues, painting the water with stunning colors. I could imagine using those colors to paint a set of nails, but I wasn't sure I'd ever be able to capture the beauty before me.

I had dreamed about the ocean thousands of times. I had read every book that I could about it, but none of that held a candle to what stood before me. As I stared out into the water, it felt like there was a world waiting just for me.

Boots crunched against the gravel, and I knew Captain Weyland was the one who stood next to me. He said nothing. Out of the corner of my eye, I saw he was staring out at the water.

"It's breathtaking," I whispered. If I talked any louder, I'd disturb the beauty before me.

The captain's gaze shifted, studying me for a long moment. "This is your first time seeing the ocean." It wasn't a question.

I nodded once. "I had told myself I would see the ocean one day, but Matron Felca always told me that pixies belonged in the forest, not in the sea. She was a respected figure, so I didn't want to break her rules. Then when she—" I cut myself off as painful memories attacked me. I cleared my throat, skipping along in my story. "Then I ended up at Ethlow and never left. I always told myself I would make it here one day, but I never thought it'd be in this way."

"The first day I saw the sea, I fell in love with it," Captain Weyland said, his voice unusually soft. "The land is weighed down by politics and rules, but on the sea, I'm the one in charge. It's just me against the world, and I'm pretty good at dancing with the wild heart of the sea." A smirk graced his features. "I could show you sometime."

For a moment, I took in the tall demon before me. There was a part of me that wanted to let go and have a real adventure with the male, but that part of me had long quieted. Messing around with Captain Weyland would only lead to heartbreak—something I wasn't sure I could handle.

"You couldn't tame me, even if you tried." I walked away, letting my hips sway and my pixie dust sparkle. I didn't dare look back at the pirate demon, even as I felt his eyes rake over my body. Despite Nyri's suggestion to have a little fun with the attractive demon, I wouldn't cross that line, especially knowing we had months of being trapped on a small ship together.

We took a rowboat to the ship where the crew met us. Captain Weyland was the first on the deck, and the crew quickly gathered to greet their captain. There were several species gathered, ranging from fae, to demon, to goblin. There was even a harpy—something Galia would love to hear about. They were all sun-kissed, but most of them had youth painting their faces, except for an old goblin that walked with a cane.

The crew quickly circled us, sizing us up. I even heard a couple of whistles. With that many eyes on me, my nerves spiked, and my pixie dust flowed in response.

"I thought you were only bringing us back a pixie. Who are these other land feeders?" A tall, muscular fae pushed through the crowd. His long, pointed ears were covered in gold piercings that matched the ring in his nose. He wasn't wearing a shirt, seemingly unbothered by the winter weather that was amplified by the sea. It revealed a large tattoo of a lion's head on his pectoral.

"They are her bodyguards," Captain Weyland said. "Don't worry. They will do their part."

Aukina and I glanced at each other. The crowd made her nervous as well, making me wonder how much information the mermaid had received about this quest and the pirate captain.

The fae looked at us, his lips curling down. "We don't need more bodies on this ship, especially two women who can't pull their weight."

Reamann stepped forward, moving between us and the fae. "That's an arrogant assumption on your part, and I'd be careful. Mermaids have pretty sharp teeth." He winked at Aukina, making her blush, before he turned back to the fae and offered his hand. "I'm Reamann, by the way. I am one of King Zathrian's guardsmen, one of the best, actually." The orange-haired demon smiled brightly, but there was an intensity in his eyes that took my breath away. He may have appeared to be all smiles, but if anyone touched the woman he loved, there was no doubt he'd run the sword strapped to his hip right through the fae's chest.

The fae smirked, delighted by the challenge. "You have a backbone, Reamann. I like it." He took the demon's hand, and the two males squeezed hard, making it look less like a handshake and more like a challenge of strength. "I am Quartermaster Alre. While you may be guests, if you do anything to endanger this crew, I won't hesitate to make you walk the plank."

"That's enough, Alre," Captain Weyland said, flaring his magic. "These are our guests, and they are under King Zathrian's protection. No harm is to come to them while on my ship."

Alre let go of Reamann's hand, but the danger in his eyes flared. "We don't follow the rules of any land demon."

"I'm your captain, and I'm giving you an order. You are not to harm a single hair on the pixie's head. If I am not enough of a threat, then you should know that the Shadow Slinger works for the king of Kinzlea. If harm comes to any of these three, it won't be me you have to face. It'll be him."

Quartermaster Alre's eyes widened slightly, but he kept his composure. He couldn't hide his face blanching, even with a smirk frozen on his face. "In that case, I will treat our guests like they are royalty."

I had heard rumors about the Shadow Slinger. He was once one of the most powerful demons in the mortal realm. Some history books even claimed he was more powerful than the five demon rulers combined, but centuries had passed since there had been any sighting of him. If the Shadow Slinger was at Ethlow, I would have known. Aukina looked just as confused as I did.

Did Captain Weyland make up a lie about the Shadow Slinger to scare his crew into not touching us?

"Stop gawking and get back to work," Captain Weyland snapped, making me jump. "You three, follow me."

None of us argued, following the captain as he gave us a brief tour of the ship, which mostly involved him pointing somewhere and telling us not to go there. We were limited to the main deck, our designated sleeping cabin, and the kitchen.

"As I said before, I expect you to pull your weight. Reamann, you can assist the crew with any physical needs, since you are clearly used to working those muscles. Ask Quartermaster Alre for your assignments daily." Reamann's face tightened at the order, but he simply nodded with acceptance. "Aukina, you are to assist the cook with whatever he needs." Aukina smiled. She loved cooking. "If you have questions, ask someone else. I have work to catch up on."

Captain Weyland walked off, his boots thunking against the wood, making his presence known to any crew member he passed.

I rushed after him. "Wait, I have a question."

"I told you to ask someone else." He didn't slow down, forcing me to move faster with my short legs.

"You didn't assign me a job."

"And?"

"You said we all need to do our part. I can help the crew." I didn't understand why he didn't give me a job.

Captain Weyland stopped, making me run into him. He turned slowly. "Your skills are not needed until we reach Dragon's Breath Island. I can't risk you and that pixie dust getting harmed before then, so relax, sunbathe, do whatever that pretty little face of yours wants, except get yourself in trouble."

"I am more than just my pixie dust, and I'm not fragile. I'm not interested in being lackadaisical on this ship. I can do my part." At Ethlow, I was constantly moving. The thought of holding still made me nervous.

Captain Weyland lifted his brows. "Lackadaisical? That's an awfully big word for such a small being."

His condescending tone made me huff. I placed my hands on my hips as I glared at him. "I know I can be an asset to you, so use me."

He hummed, rubbing his jawline. "If you want something to do, you can use your assets to warm my bed."

My hands dropped, shock running through my chest. "I didn't mean it like that. I'm not interested in you."

"When you change your mind, you know where to find me." Captain Weyland winked before walking away, his footsteps silent against the deck.

Chapter 9

I unpacked my belongings in the space that was supposed to be mine for the next couple of months. It was smaller than my room at Ethlow, and the bed felt like it was a bag of sand. A damp smell lingered in the air, making my nose wrinkle. The living quarters were almost enough to make me want to go back to the demon king's estate, but I didn't like breaking promises.

King Zathrian needed me, and I was determined not to fail him. The safety of Ethlow relied on this quest, and I thought about all of those who dwelled at the demon king's estate because they were like me and had nowhere else to go. Without Ethlow, they would face a life of misery and pain.

Three knocks echoed against my open door. "How are you settling in?" Aukina asked, hovering in the doorway.

I smiled at the mermaid. We had talked here and there at Ethlow, and I saw her nearly daily, since she was in charge of the kitchen. Despite that, I didn't know much about her. "As good as I think I can."

Aukina giggled. "These spaces are tiny. I don't know how Reamann and I are going to share a bed, especially when he turns into his demon form."

I nodded, thinking about how they would fit. Aukina was short, but she was curvy like me, and when in his demon form, Reamann was taller and thicker.

"I don't envy you sharing a bed." I shook my head, smiling.

Aukina shrugged. "Even if it's a tight fit, I prefer being around him. He makes me feel safe." There were stars in her eyes. It was the kind of love I always wanted, but I feared I'd never find that connection.

"You're so lucky. I'm jealous." I laughed to make the comment feel light-hearted. While a pang of envy hit my chest, I was happy the mermaid had found love, and my lack of love life didn't change that.

"I know." She twirled a piece of her hair around. "You're not seeing anyone, are you?"

I shook my head. If I had been in a relationship, Aukina would have known. All of Ethlow would have with the way rumors spread. "No. No one has really called out to me at Ethlow. Sometimes I wonder if that's in the cards for me."

"It is. You're too sweet for that not to happen." A moment of silence hung between us as I thought about her words, wishing they were true. Aukina grabbed my hand. "Come on. Let's explore the ship. I don't want to be stuffed down here for another second."

Aukina and I walked through the deck, arm in arm. Kinzlea was a speck in the distance, and in a matter of a few hours, it would disappear altogether, leaving us with nothing but the sea. Being in the middle of the water with nowhere to go was strangely freeing. There were no walls to keep me contained.

There wasn't anything to stop the brisk air from cutting through my coat, either. I had expected it to be cold, but this was a different level. Aukina didn't seem to mind the chill, but heat radiated off her body like a furnace.

"It's been years since I've been to the sea," Aukina said. She looked out at the water with longing in her eyes.

"I've never been to the sea before," I said. If it wasn't freezing, I would've been tempted to take a dip in the water.

"Really? Aren't you a century old?"

"I will be a week after the winter solstice. When I lived with my flock, we never left the forest. Then after everything, I went to Ethlow and haven't left."

"What happened to your flock?" Aukina stared at me with big, sad eyes.

I smiled through the pain. "They are no longer with us."

Aukina squeezed my arm. "I'm so sorry."

I didn't let my smile fade, knowing if I let it drop, the tears would come. "I miss them, but I have to believe everything happens for a reason."

"It's nice to believe that, but sometimes it's hard when good people die. I can't imagine a reason for that." Aukina's voice was tight, making me wonder if she had lost someone recently. There was so much about the mermaid I didn't know.

"If everything hadn't happened, I wouldn't have been at Ethlow, which meant I wouldn't have been able to help Zathrian obtain this artifact." As terrifying as it had been to leave Ethlow, it had given me a purpose, one I had lost two decades ago. "If I stop believing that everything happens for a reason, then the world becomes a lot darker."

"That's an awfully naïve way of looking at the world." Captain Weyland leaned against the railing of the quarterdeck, looking down at where Aukina and I had been walking.

"I like to think it's optimistic." I covered my eyes to block the sun as I looked up at the captain.

"Sometimes bad things happen because bad people want to do bad things. It doesn't mean there is a reason for everything." His tone was flat, but he watched me with curiosity.

"Even bad people have good in them," I said. "Even if you don't understand their reasoning for their transgressions, it doesn't mean they are pure evil."

Captain Weyland huffed. "You love to use big words, Sunshine." He rubbed his jawline, a smirk crossing his lips.

Warmth bloomed in my chest from his nickname for me. "Do I need to use simpler words for you to understand?"

"Don't worry. I can extrapolate your meanings just fine. I simply don't agree. If you're always believing the best in people, someone is bound to take advantage of you." His wink sent a shiver down my spine. There was something about his tone that implied something different.

"Don't listen to him," Aukina said. She tugged on my arm, encouraging me to walk away from him. "He's probably just jaded."

Captain Weyland chuckled at the mermaid's comment. "Don't forget, you're on a pirate ship. We don't like to play by the rules."

I glanced back at the captain, and his silver eye flashed when we made eye contact. Even with his warning about pirates, I couldn't believe the captain was all bad. He was helping King Zathrian save Ethlow, after all.

Chapter

10

After days of doing nothing, I stared out at the ocean, boredom creeping into my mind. At first, it had almost been relaxing to not have any responsibilities on the ship. At Ethlow, I never stopped moving, and there were days I wished I had more time to relax. Now that I had all the time in a day to do nothing, I wished for something, anything, to do.

I scanned the deck for the quartermaster. He was easy to find as he yelled at a lower ranked crew member for messing something up. My heart thumped as I thought about approaching the fae. I hadn't seen him say a friendly word to any of the crew members, but maybe it'd be different with me. I was the special guest.

I lingered nearby, waiting for him to finish yelling. It gave me too much time to question my choices, and I debated about finding someone else to ask for work, but my indecisiveness made me hesitate too long.

"Do you make a habit of eavesdropping on others?" Alre snapped.

My spine straightened, knowing I wasn't about to answer that question, especially when the answer was yes. "I was hoping I could assist the crew. I haven't been assigned a job, but I have plenty of skills."

Alre's eyes widened slightly. "Did Captain Weyland ask you to work?"

"No."

"Then I have nothing for you."

I pursed my lips, but I wasn't about to give up. "There has to be something I can help with. I'm going crazy. There's nothing to do on this ship except sit around and contemplate life, and I might throw myself overboard if I have to do that."

Alre smiled at that. "That desperate, huh?" I nodded once. "I might have something you can do." He looked up, and my eyes followed his gaze to the crow's nest. "No one has cleaned up there for a long time, and I'm sure it's covered in bird shit. If you are insistent on doing something, you can do that, unless you are too delicate to do work like that." He leaned forward, a challenge raging in his eyes.

"I can handle work." I resisted the urge to look at the height of the crow's nest, not wanting the quartermaster to see my hesitation.

A sinister smile tainted Alre's face. "There is a bucket and a scraper over there." He gestured behind me. "Glad we finally found a use for you."

I forced a smile back at him. "I'm happy to help."

I grabbed the supplies before moving to the rope ladder that went all the way to the crow's nest. It was hooked to the mast every several feet to prevent the wind from blowing it wildly, but that didn't stop the invisible force from whipping it around. I took several long breaths, telling myself it was fine. If it was dangerous, the quartermaster wouldn't have risked my safety, not when the quest couldn't be completed without me.

I hooked the bucket over my arm before I began the journey up. The first several steps had my heart racing. The ladder was more stable than it looked, which was one of the reasons I kept climbing. The other was because I could feel Alre watching me, and I wasn't about to chicken out, not after I insisted I could be useful. When I was about halfway up, my lungs burned, partially from the exercise, but more so from my rapid breath that had little to do with the strength it took to climb.

Don't look down.

I told myself that on repeat. I kept my eyes forward, glancing up occasionally to see how much farther it was. My hands ached from the rope rubbing them raw, but I had gone too far to give up. When I finally reached the crow's nest, I hauled myself onto the solid structure, and relief washed over me.

Until I looked down.

The ship below looked unnervingly small, and one wrong move would result in me splattering to the ground. I dropped to my hands and knees, but it didn't stop the world from spinning or my chest from tightening. My fingers pressed into the boards beneath me, a reminder I was safe. I was on solid ground. Sort of. I glanced at the bucket, knowing I had to push past my fear and do the work I said I would, or else no one would take me seriously. I didn't want my only use on this ship to be my pixie dust.

I was safe. Being high up didn't change that.

My pixie dust filled the air before falling onto the bucket and scraper. The metal floated into the air, and I quickly snatched it before it floated where I couldn't grab it. I shifted onto my butt and clung to the bucket. The distraction helped, but I knew I couldn't look down again if I had any chance of doing the job assigned to me.

I didn't know how much time had passed as I scraped bird poop off the railing of the crow's nest while strategically looking anywhere but down. My arm ached, but I was determined to keep going until I was done. The last thing I wanted to do was come back up the next day.

When the ache in my arm became too much, I sat down to take a slight break. The flapping of wings pulled my attention as a crow circled above my head. After days of traveling on the sea, we were far from any land, so it was strange for a crow to be near the ship. The black birds weren't fans of the sea, from what I had read.

"You're far from home."

Caw! The bird swooped down, landing on part of the clean railing. It tilted its head as it looked at me.

"I guess I'm far from home, too," I said. The word home tasted bittersweet. Ethlow had become home in every sense of the word, but it wasn't the life I had imagined. "I'm not really sure what I'm doing here, honestly. I want to help King Zathrian, but this feels above my head. I can't even climb the crow's nest without a panic attack." I shook my head, wondering why I was talking to a bird. Maybe it was because I could express my doubts without judgment or fear of it coming back to bite me. "I guess I wanted to feel useful, because then it means there was a reason I survived when my flock died. If I can do good in the world, then it wouldn't hurt so much to know I survived when they didn't."

Caw! The tone sounded mocking, which I didn't think was possible for a bird.

I narrowed my eyes. "You don't have the right to judge me, not when you're probably the one shitting up here." I wasn't one to let profanities slip from my mouth on a regular basis, but it wasn't like the bird understood what I was saying.

Caw! Caw! The crow took off, and then I felt something splash on my shoulder. Horror flowed through me as I took in the bird poop on my shirt. My mouth fell open at the clear insult. Maybe the bird understood what I was saying, after all.

"Thanks," I muttered under my breath, making a mental note to be extra nice the next time I came across a crow.

I pushed through the rest of the cleaning, desperate to take a bath—if that was a possibility. I had used the washroom to relieve myself, but I had yet to use it to wash up. It hadn't been urgent until a crow used me as a toilet.

The moment I finished, I moved to the ladder. I looked down, and my stomach sank. Going down felt a million times harder. I should have chickened out the moment Alre challenged me. Pride be damned if I was going to die up there.

I bit my lip, knowing I would die up there if I didn't suck up my fear and push through. Slowly, very slowly, I put my foot down, wiggling it until I found the first rung of the ladder. I put my weight on it, barely breathing. My hands ached even more after hours of scraping the railing clean. I didn't have a choice if I wanted to get back to the deck of the ship, so I focused on taking it one step at a time.

I was a little more than halfway down when a gust of wind hit the ship, making the ladder shake. I clung to the rope with all of my strength, a blood-curdling scream escaping my mouth. I dropped the bucket, barely hearing the metal slam against the floor below. My eyes shut tight, and my lungs refused to work. The muscles in my entire body were rigid. The wind whipped the rope again, shaking the entire thing.

Commotion erupted below me, but I couldn't hear any distinct words being shouted over the thrumming of my heart.

I was going to die on the ladder.

My brain had convinced me of that, and there was nothing that was going to change my mind. My muscles would give out, and I would fall to the ground with nothing but wood to catch me. If my wings worked, I would have been fine, but I hadn't used them in twenty years, and I didn't trust them to save me.

"Elcy!" Captain Weyland's voice cut through the pounding in my head. He was livid, not concerned.

I couldn't respond to him. I couldn't even open my eyes. I was frozen, clinging to the rope for fear of my life.

"What are you doing?" he demanded, the irritation in his voice growing.

"I can't get down." I didn't know if he heard me over the wind, but speaking at all was a feat.

"Just fly down."

"I can't." My voice broke on the last word. I waited for Captain Weyland to yell at me or scold me.

The ladder shook, and a whimper escaped my mouth. I tried to control my breath, but nothing I did helped.

Something touched my ankle, and I nearly let go as I shrieked.

"Elcy." Captain Weyland's deep voice filled my ears. It was steady and calm, opposite to my racing heart. I wanted to look down to see if it was him grabbing my ankle, but I couldn't open my eyes. "Elcy, you need to climb down."

"I can't. I'm scared." I waited for his laugh. A pixie afraid of heights? It was a ridiculous thought.

"I'm right here. I won't let you fall." His voice cut through the pounding in my head. His warmth caressed my leg, and I knew I could trust him.

"I can't." I wanted to climb down. I wanted my feet safely on the ground again, but my muscles had cramped, and fear held me hostage.

Captain Weyland grunted. "You are a bigger pain in my ass than I expected."

"Too bad you need me," I snapped back. I didn't want to be a burden. This all started because I wanted to help.

"What part of stay out of trouble didn't you understand?"

I gritted my teeth. Now wasn't the time for him to scold me, not when my life hung in the balance. "Maybe I would've stayed out of trouble if you didn't treat me like I was useless."

"You're not useless." His voice was sharper as he said that. "You are precious, which is why I need you to climb down."

My hands shook. I knew I couldn't hold on much longer. "I'm scared." I was repeating myself, but I couldn't help it.

Captain Weyland grunted again. The ladder shook as he reached up, grabbing a rung near my midsection. There wasn't enough space for the two of us, but that didn't stop him from hauling himself higher. The demon leaned off to the side, holding the ladder with one hand. He wrapped his free arm around my waist and held me against him.

"I won't let any harm come to you." His deep voice caressed my ear, making me feel safe. "Hold on to me, and I'll get you down."

"I'm too heavy to carry." The insecurity spilled out of my mouth without a thought. The fear of falling had torn through my usual filters.

"Listen to me, Sunshine. You are not too heavy. Now let go."

His command snapped something inside of me, and I let go of the rope, squeaking as I did. I clung to his neck, my heart going wild. Captain Weyland didn't let go of me, holding both of our weight with ease.

The captain readjusted, and then he loosened his grip on the side of the rope ladder, allowing him to slide down with me in his arms. As his feet hit the ground, it sounded like thunder ringing out.

I cracked my eyes open, realizing we were safely on the ground. Nearly the entire crew had gathered to watch the ordeal, and heat crawled up my neck, knowing they all had just witnessed that.

I started to let go of Captain Weyland's neck, but he tightened his grip on me.

"You're not going anywhere yet, not until we have a proper talk in my office." Captain Weyland moved through the crowd, the crew parting the second he walked towards them.

Alre winked at me and mouthed the words, "Good luck," making my stomach twist in a different way. That wasn't going to be a fun conversation.

Chapter

II

Light orbs illuminated Captain Weyland's office. Shelves lined the walls filled with books, scrolls of paper, and other various odds and ends. A large desk sat on the side of the room, and an armchair with a table was tucked in the corner. A melted candle indicated many long nights had been spent in that corner. The use of a candle intrigued me when there were magic orbs to illuminate the room. Only non-magical beings had to rely on candles.

The captain moved through his office towards a second door. On the other side, there was another room that was large. Unlike his office, there were paintings with gold frames decorating the walls. The bed in the center could fit three bodies with space in between, the exact opposite of the stiff mattresses in the crew quarters. The sheets were made of dark red silk, and a fur carpet lay in the center of the floor.

Captain Weyland lowered me to my feet, but he kept his hands on my hips. "Are you okay?"

My lip wobbled as the adrenaline wore off. Now that I was safe, my emotions overflowed. I clenched my jaw, willing for the tears to stay back. I couldn't cry in front of Captain Weyland. He already

THE DEMON KING'S TEACHER

thought I was pathetic, and I couldn't risk making him think worse of me.

I couldn't speak to him. Even a single word would make the tears fall freely.

Captain Weyland knelt on the ground, making it so we were nearly eye level. "You are safe."

I blinked, and two large tears rolled down my face. My breath was shaky. I was safe, but my body hadn't caught up with that knowledge. For a moment, I had thought I was going to die.

"You are safe," he repeated. His words caressed my nerves, calming them.

"I don't want to go back up there," I whispered, unsure if I'd be able to speak any louder.

"You shouldn't have been up there in the first place." The bite in his tone made my chest clench. I understood why he was angry. I ignored his orders and ended up causing trouble for him.

"I asked Alre to give me work, because I was going stir crazy. I didn't expect for him to ask me to climb up to the crow's nest." It was no one's fault but my own.

"Alre asked you to go up there?" He stood, his demeanor making me flinch. I couldn't imagine the captain hurting me, but I was aware there wasn't much I could do to stop him if he tried.

"But I'm the one who agreed. If you're mad at anyone, it should be me." The last thing I wanted to do was get Alre in trouble. It wasn't like he asked me to go up to the crow's nest with ill intention. He probably thought it wouldn't have been an issue for me because of my wings.

"I *am* mad at you." The declaration hurt worse than I thought. "If you had slipped and died, then all of this would have been for nothing."

I sank onto his bed. The feather-stuffed mattress was a thousand times more comfortable than what I had been sleeping on. "You only care about my pixie dust." I didn't know what I was expecting. It wasn't like the captain had shown any interest in me other than casual flirtations.

"Are you disappointed by that?" His face was unreadable. With how attractive the captain was, I was sure he had men and women falling all over him. A short, overweight pixie wasn't enough to pull the attention of someone like him—not that I wanted his attention.

"No." The hollowness in my chest said otherwise, but I tried to ignore it. He wasn't the relationship kind, and I wasn't the one-night stand kind of woman.

Captain Weyland stalked towards me. He pressed his hands on the bed on either side of me, bringing his face inches away from mine. "I told you I'd be happy to have you warm my bed. I'd even make your legs quake so you wouldn't be tempted to disobey my orders again."

I licked my lips, all too aware of the lack of space between us. I leaned back, but there was nowhere to go. "I don't spread my legs for just anyone."

"You could be a good girl and spread them for me." His smirk only added to his words.

I squirmed beneath him, trying to ignore what the suggestion did to my body. "No, thank you."

"Then I want you to tell me what happened up there."

I took a shaky breath, but it felt like there wasn't enough oxygen in the room. I wasn't sure which conversation scared me more. "You already know what happened."

"No, I don't. I know you were afraid, but I don't understand. With your wings, it should have been easy for you to fly down." He didn't break eye contact, refusing to give me any room to back out of the conversation.

"I was scared and wasn't thinking." I definitely wanted to go back to the conversation of warming his bed.

"Don't give me that. Why didn't you fly?"

My heart thundered, fear striking me all over again. I didn't want to tell Captain Weyland the truth, because I didn't want him to think less of me. I didn't want to lie, either.

"I... I can't."

He blinked. "You can't, or you won't?"

My wings buzzed from nerves, making my pixie dust spill onto the bed. "I can't."

"They don't appear to be damaged." He hadn't taken his eyes off me, yet he was confident in his statement. When had he studied my wings?

I couldn't think of a lie to distract him with, which left me with the truth. "According to healers, there is nothing wrong with them, but I haven't been able to fly in twenty years."

He cocked an eyebrow. "Why?"

That was a question I had asked myself countless times. "I don't know."

"What happened?"

I gritted my teeth. Why wouldn't he let it go? I wanted to walk away, but his body trapped me on his bed. "Why does it matter?"

"Because if there is nothing physically wrong, that means it's all in your head." He tapped his finger against my forehead. "If we're going to get you flying again, we have to break through that barrier."

"Maybe I can't fly anymore." It was a fear I hadn't spoken out loud before.

Captain Weyland grabbed my chin, tilting my head up. His eyes flicked to my lips, making me wonder what he'd taste like.

"Aren't you the one who is supposed to believe anyone can do anything?" His tone was condescending, but it was difficult to focus on as his scent swarmed over me.

I turned my head away, breaking free from his grasp. I was afraid that if I kept facing him, all of my secrets would come undone. "Can we get this artifact without me flying?"

Captain Weyland straightened, the moment between us passing in an instant. "Technically, yes."

"Then it doesn't matter if I can't fly." I stood and put more distance between us. "I won't cause you any more trouble, and when we reach the island, I'll be here to assist."

"Elcy." His tone made me tense. "If I have anything to say about it, you will be flying before you go back home."

"You're wasting your time."

"Not with you. There's something special inside of you, and I intend to break it free." His gaze was unfaltering, which made my heart warm. It had been a long time since someone told me there was something special in me. It was almost too much to think about.

"I should go. I probably smell awful." It was more of an excuse than anything, but I became painfully aware of the bird poop on my shirt and how I had been clinging to Captain Weyland while blubbering.

"Use my washroom. It'll be better than the one in the common quarters, and then there is no risk of someone walking in on you naked, since you seem to have a habit of that." He gestured to a curtain on the other side of the room.

My mouth gaped open, unsure of what to take from that. Did he care if others saw me naked, or did he think that little of me? I was tempted to tell him no from pride, but the common washroom had an unpleasant smell to it.

"Fine, but you better not peek." I walked towards the separate room.

"If I wanted to see you naked, I wouldn't have to resort to tacky methods. I could have you writhing on my bed with only a few words."

His statement was bold, and I tried to tell myself he was wrong, but the slickness between my legs said otherwise.

I slipped into the washroom, not trusting myself to stay near the pirate demon a moment longer. I was surprised to find a tub large enough for two with running hot water. I hadn't expected the luxury of hot water on the sea, but that was the advantage of having a demon as a pirate captain. King's Zathrian's magic kept Ethlow running, so I was sure it was Captain Weyland's magic I had to thank for the steaming bath.

I washed as quickly as possible, using the soap that smelled of roses with gold flecks embedded in the bar. By the time I was done, a wave of exhaustion washed over me. Having a panic attack while clinging to a rope ladder had drained my energy levels. That mixed with a warm bath made the call of sleep ring loudly. If Weyland hadn't been on the other side of the curtain, it would have been easy to fall asleep in the bath, but knowing he was a few feet away kept me on edge.

As I dried off, I noticed a fresh set of clothes sitting on a small table. I hadn't seen them when I first entered, but I had also been focused on scrubbing off the day. The clothes looked and smelled like the captain, so I was sure I was too round for them to fit, but the only other options were to enter his room in a towel—something I refused to do—or put on the clothes covered in bird poop. Also not an option.

As I pulled on the new clothes, I was surprised to find that the shirt fit with room to spare. It draped down to my knees, covering my body like a dress, so I didn't bother with the pants. When I stepped out of the washroom, Captain Weyland sat on his bed with several papers laid out before him. Maps of various sizes, style, and color filled the pages, but the moment I stepped out of the washroom, the captain gathered the paper.

My curiosity piqued, but I wasn't in a place to press for details. "Thank you for the bath, but I should get going."

Captain Weyland turned, taking me in. My hair dripped down onto the shirt I borrowed. As he looked me up and down, a low growl escaped his lips. "I'm not sure how I feel about you in my clothes."

I looked down, knowing the male shirt wasn't flattering like my own clothes. It didn't emphasize my curves the way I liked. I tucked a piece of hair behind my ear, insecurities washing over me. "I didn't want to put on the other shirt, since it smelled. I will return this to you as soon as I can."

He moved closer. "You misunderstand. I *like* the way you look in my clothes."

My breath hitched. I wasn't used to males hitting on me. I wasn't thin, and I wasn't the standard of beauty. While I liked the curves my breasts and hips gave me, I wished they were smaller. But the way the captain's eyes grazed over my skin made me feel beautiful and wanted.

What would it have felt like to give into temptation and forget about the consequences? To indulge in a night of pleasure that meant nothing to either party?

I quickly tossed that thought to the side. I knew myself well enough to know that I couldn't keep the heart and the body separate.

"Good night, Weyland." I slipped out of his room before I could question why I dropped his title or change my mind and dive into dangerous waters.

Chapter
12

A loud knock woke me from a deep sleep the next morning. I looked around, forgetting where I was for a moment, but the slight rocking of the ship and the sound of crashing waves outside my window brought it all back. I rubbed the crusties from my eyes and stretched my arms above my head, groaning at the ache in my muscles. I never wanted to climb another rope ladder again.

Three more knocks rang out, less patient than before. I forced myself out of bed and cracked the door open. Captain Weyland stood on the other side.

He took in my messy hair and disheveled appearance. I was still in his shirt from the day before. By the time I had made it back to my room, I had been too tired to change. I should have taken a moment to gussy up, but I hadn't thought about who would be on the other side.

"Get dressed. You're coming with me." His voice was colder than it had been last night. Was he upset because I rejected his advances?

"Where are we going?"

"Get dressed," he repeated.

I shut the door and quickly changed, opting for a simple pair of pants and a thick sweater. The open deck was brisk with winter winds, and there wasn't anything to block the cold from chilling me to my bones. The moment I left the room, Captain Weyland moved without a word. I had to jog to keep up with him. We climbed the stairs to the deck, and a blast of wind hit me. I wrapped my arms around myself, wishing I had bothered to grab a jacket.

Captain Weyland stopped when he reached the upper deck. The few crew members that had been relaxing up there quickly scattered at the sight of their captain. He was a feared pirate, even among his own crew. He clasped his hands behind his back, looking out at the ocean.

"If we're going to figure this out, you have to tell me what happened twenty years ago." His voice was clear, even with the wind whipping around us.

"Figure what out?" I asked slowly. My lungs ached from the quick movement, but I didn't want him to know that.

"Why there is a disconnect between your head and your wings." Captain Weyland turned to face me. "I told you I would help you fly again, and I don't go back on my word."

"You're still going to help me? I thought you'd be petulant after last night." I had barely slept since I ran out of the captain's room, avoiding his advances. He seemed like the type of male that was used to getting what he wanted, and most males like that didn't take rejection well.

"Petulant?" the captain repeated. "Do you like using fancy words to make yourself feel intelligent?"

I huffed and rolled my eyes, pressing my forearms against the railing of the ship. "I am the teacher at Ethlow. I'm expected to be educated, but I also like words. It's difficult to express oneself without the proper phrasing. I could have said I thought you'd be angry, but angry is such a bland word. Petulance is what I expected."

I wanted to ask him if he was upset about the way I ran away from him, but the words fell to the pit of my stomach. I didn't want to know, no matter what his response was.

Captain Weyland leaned next to me, his back to the ocean. "I have no reason to be petulant. I am vexed, but that's because you won't tell me why you can't fly."

"I'm sure you have your secrets. Can't this be mine?"

He didn't respond immediately, and when he finally spoke, it wasn't what I had expected. "Do you know why I chose the seas instead of staying on land?"

I studied the demon for a moment. Piracy was idealized on land. There were stories about treasure and adventure, love and fighting. It was better than the grueling nature of day-to-day life, but I knew it was a fantasy. Being on a ship away from the land for months at a time meant limited fresh food and being stuck in the same small space with the same crew members. Someone who chose life at sea either had no choice, or it was deeper than that.

"The sea calls to you," I answered.

Captain Weyland huffed. "Maybe you're smarter than I gave you credit for."

I narrowed my eyes. "What's that supposed to mean?"

He waved his hand, brushing off the comment. "You're right. The sea calls to me in a way most can't understand. It's a part of me. He lifted his hand, and the waves crashing against the ship responded, pulling higher out of the sea than they had a moment prior. A surge of power filled the air.

"You can control water with your magic?" I gasped. All demons had a magical element to them. Some of the weaker ones had abnormal strength, while the more powerful demons could control various elements. The unique ones could control aspects of the world, like shadows and light.

"Not water. The sea," Captain Weyland corrected. "I have mild control over fresh-water, like lakes, but the sea bends to my will. That is the reason I am king of the sea. While out here, no one can defeat me, not even the five demons who claim kingdoms on the land. That's why Zathrian made a deal with me to retrieve this artifact. He knew he needed me on his side instead of as his enemy."

He pushed up his sleeve, revealing a dark black tattoo in the shape of two horns that overlapped. I hadn't seen the demon king's signet before, but the mark burned into the captain's arm had the essence of King Zathrian emitting from it. It was a reminder that King Zathrian was a demon, and demons had to make deals to increase their powers and control others.

"And what does this have to do with getting my wings to work again?"

"Because, Sunshine, Zathrian asked you to help him with this incredibly dangerous and important task. He only asked those who he thought were absolutely necessary and qualified. If the king of Kinzlea can put his faith in a little pixie like you, then you can put your faith in yourself. You don't want to talk about your past? Fine, but you have to believe in yourself, or nothing will come out of this training."

"I believe in myself." As the words came out of my mouth, I knew they weren't true. The look Captain Weyland gave me told me he didn't believe me either.

Everything Captain Weyland and I tried over the next week failed. I was no closer to flying than before. I moved my wings, but they wouldn't move at the speed needed for takeoff. My pixie dust flowed from my wings, but not at the velocity necessary to fly. For my wings to deny gravity, they required a delicate balance of pixie dust and speed.

The captain tried words of encouragement and words of fear. He tried to get me to talk about my past, but my lips were sealed on that topic. Telling him I only survived because I snuck away from my flock wouldn't change anything that happened. It wouldn't bring back those I once loved or my ability to fly.

Then the captain moved on to physical methods. He had me stand on the railing and told me to jump—that had only worked in making me cry. Today, we went through a series of exercises I had seen warriors do at Ethlow while training. By the end of it, I was too exhausted to try flying.

"That's enough for today," Captain Weyland said.

Drops of sweat collected on my forehead. The winter chill clung to the air, but there was a strange lack of wind. It didn't stop the ship from propelling forward at a speed that should have been impossible without the wind catching the sails.

"How is any of this going to help me fly?" It was a genuine question. I didn't understand how the repetitive physical regimen would get my wings to work. As I waited for a reply, I sank to the ground and sat cross-legged. My legs ached too much to stand.

"I hoped exhausting you would stop you from overthinking, and you'd let go of whatever trauma you're holding onto."

I winced at his bluntness. That night haunted my dreams, but I didn't let it rule me. I tried to spread positivity wherever I could. I didn't want to live my life in fear, but I hadn't been living much at all.

"I'm too tired to move, so your plan backfired."

"Do you need me to carry you back to your bed, Sunshine?" His smirk drove me crazy.

I tried not to think about the demon pirate that way, but it had grown increasingly more difficult to push away those thoughts, especially after spending time with him daily to help me. It wasn't like he needed my flying abilities, especially with a harpy on his crew. He was helping me for my sake, which cracked my heart open.

It was a dangerous and exhilarating thought.

"I can walk." I shifted to push to my feet, but Captain Weyland was there in an instant. He took my hand and pulled me up with ease. My aching thighs were grateful for the assistance.

"The offer to carry you is still open." He held onto my hand for longer than what was necessary, but I didn't pull away, not as the scent of the sea mixed with cedarwood caressed my nose.

"I don't think the crew would respect me if they saw you carrying me. They already look at me like a nuisance." Aukina and Reamann were the only ones I talked to besides the captain. The others avoided me like I had the plague.

"They are just worried about facing my wrath." Captain Weyland took his hat off, finally releasing my hand. His dark hair fell around his horns and ears, brushing against his shoulders. The strip of white dangled in front of his black eye.

"And why would they face your wrath?" I lifted my brows.

"Because I told them that if anyone pulled a stunt like Alre with you again, they would walk the plank and find a very unforgiving sea beneath them." His silver and black eyes hardened, a coldness washing through his face.

The threat should have scared me, but no one had acted so protective of me before. I knew King Zathrian had told him to keep me safe, but this felt almost possessive.

Before I could respond, a crack resounded through the air. Captain Weyland rushed to the railing, snapping his hat back into place. I was by him a moment later, my eyes widening at the ship quickly approaching. They had a gold flag with a black hourglass painted on the surface. A gust of wind hit my face out of nowhere, and the smell of gunpowder burned my nose.

"Get to your cabin now, and don't come out until I tell you it's safe," Captain Weyland snapped.

"Why? Who is that?" My heart rate increased at the intensity of the captain's voice.

"The one pirate in all the seas deranged enough to take me on, and if my inkling is right, she's here to steal my treasure, which is why I need you to hide. Now."

Another cannon fired, splashing in the water nearly close enough to hit me. Captain Weyland didn't have to tell me a second time before I took off running.

Chapter 13

The ship erupted into chaos as Captain Weyland and Quartermaster Alre shouted orders. A flurry of bodies moved to their practice positions with ease. It was as if everyone had rehearsed thousands of times to make the transition seamless. Several crew members bumped into me as I tried to make my way to the cabin. I tucked my wings in tight, afraid they'd get damaged in the commotion.

"Elcy!" Aukina rushed over to me and grabbed my hands. "Thank Artagatis you're okay."

I held onto her, relieved to see the mermaid safe. "Captain Weyland told me to get below deck and stay there until this is over. Let's go." I tried to pull the mermaid, but she dug her feet in.

"I can't hide, not when I can help." Her face was tight, and it was clear her mind was made up.

"But it's dangerous." I wished I was the type to fight, but I knew I wasn't. I had spent the last twenty years hiding away at Ethlow instead of fighting to make sure those who attacked my flock got the punishment they deserved.

"I'm not worried. I've been training with Reamann. Besides, I'm unstoppable in the water." She squeezed my hand and smiled, her eyes glimmering with excitement. "But you hide. We need to keep you safe." She let go and took off running into the action. She met up with Reamann, who was tying a rope. Touching her mate's shoulder, she said something that was lost in a cannon explosion. Reamann kept his hands busy as he said something back. Aukina took a step back, but he grabbed her, pulling her into a quick kiss before they both went their separate ways.

My stomach twisted as I focused on hiding. Bodies rushed up and down the stairs that led to the cabin to reach the cannons below deck. The crew quarters were on the level below that, and I knew I'd have to push through the fray to hide. My chest tightened as I moved towards the stairs. I wanted to help, but without proper training, I'd get in the way. Hiding was better than hindering the crew, even if it made me feel like a coward.

Before I made it five steps, Alre caught my arm. "You don't want to go down there."

"Captain Weyland gave me orders to hide in the cabins." I thought bringing up the captain's name would have been enough to make the fae let go, but he kept his grip firm.

"Do you see those cannons aimed at us?" Alre gestured to the ship that was shifting its position to line up with the side of Captain Weyland's ship. "When it gets close enough, those cannon balls are going to rip through the sides of the ships, likely where you are hiding in your cabin."

A knot formed in my throat. "Why would Captain Weyland tell me to go down there, then?" I didn't think the captain would want me hurt.

"He probably wasn't thinking. There's a lot going on." As if to emphasize Alre's point, another cannon fired, frighteningly close to the ship.

"Then where am I supposed to hide?" I looked around, but the deck was open and filled with chaos.

"Go to the captain's office. You'll be safer there." Alre released my arm and didn't waste time springing into action.

Captain Weyland's office was on the same level as the deck, making it easy to navigate to. I didn't wait for additional orders. As I reached the door, a cannon ball struck the railing, making the ship sway. I lost my balance and slammed into the door. My shoulder throbbed, but I didn't have time to worry about it. I scrambled for the handle and pushed the door open as another boom rang out.

I slammed the door shut behind me and rushed to the captain's desk, tucking myself into the space beneath. My body trembled as I listened to the explosions and screams outside. Pixie dust poured off my wings, making the air around me glow. I felt helpless and useless, and I hated not knowing what was happening outside. I hated knowing I was the only one hiding.

Each explosion made my muscles tense more and brought me closer to tears. I placed my hands over my ears and took a deep breath. As I exhaled, I let a song slip from my mouth. It was the song Matron Felca used to sing to us around the campfire when we were getting ready to wind down for the night. I hadn't sung it since arriving at Ethlow, but the lyrics flowed from my mouth with ease as it tumbled out of the depths of my memory.

The song had always soothed me, even if the matron's voice was raw and often cracked. The smooth, lilting rhythm had lulled me to sleep on countless nights, and now it slowed my heart rate, making the explosions fade into the distance.

As I finished the song, I dragged my hands away from my ears, hoping the chaos outside had ceased. The door to the captain's office slammed open, making me yelp. I started climbing out, hoping it was Captain Weyland coming to get me to tell me it was safe.

"I know you're in here, little pixie. Come out now, and you won't get hurt." The deep male voice was unfamiliar to me. It was possible he was part of the crew. There were too many beings on the ship, and with most of them avoiding me, it was impossible to talk to all of them. However, the tone of his voice slithered down my spine in a way that gave me the ick.

I tucked myself back under the desk with careful movements and held my breath. My heart pounded in my ears, but I hoped I was the only one who could hear it.

"You're only going to make this more difficult for yourself." Multiple sets of boots clicked against the floor. An explosion rang out, and I threw my hand over my mouth to stop the cry from escaping, but it had only muffled it.

The footsteps stopped, and my breath grew ragged.

A head appeared in front of me, and I couldn't control the scream that wracked my body. The male's pale skin made him look sickly, and his thin, unwashed hair only added to it. His breath smelled like death, forcing me to cover my mouth.

He grabbed my arm, dragging me out from underneath the desk. There were two fae with him that towered over his frail elven form. He dug his fingers into my arm so hard there would be bruises there later.

"Let go!" I shouted. Any attempt at fighting was pointless. There was a small chance I could take him down, but I stood no chance against the fae next to him. Their powers made the room suffocating.

"Not a chance. Captain Irelina expects your presence on her ship." The elf pinched the tip of my wing, making me go deathly still. "That's what I thought," he said in my ear. "If you fight or scream, I will tear your wing, and you'll never be able to fly again."

My throat went dry. I couldn't fly now, but if Captain Weyland was correct, it was because of a mental block. If the elf ripped my wing, there was no fixing that, especially not on the seas.

"That's what I thought. You'll come with us quickly and quietly, if you want to maintain those pretty wings of yours." He pulled me along, keeping his grip as tight as before.

I didn't dare say a single word, and my feet moved as quickly as they could. As we left the captain's office, a cannonball struck the ship, causing splinters to fly and the ship to rock. The only reason I stayed on my feet was because of the grip on my arm. For as peaked as he looked, he was surprisingly strong.

Sounds of metal clanging rolled over the deck. Enemies had invaded the ship, and crew members fought viciously against them. I recognized at least half of the crew members, but there were several pairings where I couldn't tell who belonged to what crew. I continued scanning, desperate to get the attention of anyone who would help.

Reamann was nowhere to be found. He was either helping with the cannons below, or something had happened to him, something I didn't want to think about. There were no signs of Aukina, but I was sure she was in the sea. Alre was on the other side of the ship, swinging on a rope and blasting ice against enemies. He was too far away to help, and I didn't dare call out and risk my wings. My last hope was Captain Weyland. I looked where I had last seen him, but he had since moved.

"Hurry up, pixie. You're dawdling on purpose." The elf yanked on my arm, and it felt like it was going to rip out of its socket.

We reached the edge of the railing where an opening had been blasted through. A rope ladder had been tied to what remained of the railing, and it led to a row boat below. I was out of time.

I glanced over my shoulder one last time, praying that anyone would see me. The elf yanked my arm, shoving me into the chest of one of the fae. It was at that moment that I caught the silver and black gaze of Captain Weyland. His body froze mid swing, and he muttered something that could have only been a profanity.

Before I could see the rest of his response, a fae yanked me off the ship. My stomach lurched as I looked at the distance below us. If I fell, it'd be into the water, but that didn't stop the fear from coursing through me. I clung to the fae carrying me down, terrified for my life. I didn't want to be on this adventure anymore. I wanted to go back to the boring life of a teacher at the demon king's estate.

I'd rather deal with paper cuts and crying children than heights and cannons and pirates.

I was shoved into the rowboat, landing hard on my bottom. I pushed myself up, my entire body shaking. Captain Weyland would come for me. He needed me, and he had made a deal with King Zathrian. He wouldn't leave me in the hands of these pirates who planned to do unknown things to me.

I watched the ship, waiting for the captain to appear. He saw them taking me. I didn't know how, but he would come swooping in and save me. If I stopped believing that for a second, I would have lost any sense of calm I had.

It became harder to stay quiet, and by the time they dragged me onto the other ship, my entire body shook with fear.

The elf chuckled, amused by my distress. "I like it when a woman quivers."

The delight in his voice sickened me. "You're the worst kind of male." I didn't know where my outburst came from. I knew better. If I kept my mouth shut, I'd stay safe a little longer. Only I couldn't stand the way the elf looked at me like I was nothing more than an object.

His hand hit my face faster than I could process. I pressed my hand against my stinging skin. I didn't know what I had expected to happen after my remark, but it wasn't that.

"You're going to regret that," I whispered.

"And what is a little pixie like you going to do? You were cowering away from the fight. I doubt you have the guts to take me on." The elf sneered. His hand looked ready to hit me again.

A screech pulled all of our attention to the sky as a harpy flew overhead. In her arms was the pirate I had become all so familiar with. She let go of the captain, and he fell to the ground, his boots hitting the deck like a clap of thunder. "It's not her you have to be afraid of."

Chapter 14

The elf went white as he saw Captain Weyland behind him. He barely had time to stumble back before the demon pirate reached out and grabbed him by the throat. "Did you think you could touch my treasure and live to see another day?" Captain Weyland slammed the elf down, cracking his head against the railing of the ship. His silver eye glimmered as sharp teeth emerged from his mouth. He slammed the elf against the railing again, and this time the male went limp.

The two fae stalked forward, their canines extending as their animalistic side came out. Captain Weyland turned to them, and his face burned with fury. His body grew larger as his skin turned gray like a stormy sky. His horns pushed his hat off his head, and power flowed from the demon pirate. The fae were no match for him, but it didn't stop them from approaching the captain with daggers covered in flames.

Captain Weyland lifted his hands, and two streams of water emerged from the sea. With a simple push, the streams slammed into the males' faces. They gurgled and clawed at their throats as sea water slammed into their mouths. Blood poured from their noses and ears as the pressure destroyed their organs.

The pirate demon didn't relent until the fae dropped to their knees. Only then did Captain Weyland drop his arms. Water tainted red drained from the males who tried to kidnap me.

Other enemy crew members hovered nearby, but after seeing the attack on their comrades, they kept their distance from Captain Weyland.

There was only one who dared to approach. Her long, red hair shifted in the wind, but her brown leather hat kept it tame. She wore knee-high boots that matched her hat. A corset layered over her flowing white shirt, making her waist look snatched. Her green eyes flared with power.

"I didn't think the dreaded Captain Weyland would dare step foot on my ship." She grinned wildly, revealing a mouth filled with sharp teeth.

"I didn't think you were stupid enough to attack me, Irelina," Captain Weyland snapped back.

"That's Captain Irelina. You may think you are the king of the sea, but I am a goddess. I was born to the sea, which is how I know you'll die to it." She winked, placing her hands on her hips.

"You're the one who is going to die in the sea. We've done this battle before, and you know who wins." Captain Weyland flared his power, making his strength known.

"You say that, yet here I am, still standing." Captain Irelina opened her arms wide. "And now you have something precious you're trying to protect. Tell me, have you fucked her yet?"

Captain Weyland snarled as if he was insulted.

The captain's response only made Irelina's eyes dance. "No? I'm shocked. That'll make my offer easier for you to accept."

The harpy who dropped Captain Weyland off at the ship landed next to him, her claws and feathers soaked with blood. Based on the feral grin on her face, the blood didn't belong to her. Even if it did, she didn't care. She lived for the fight.

"Quinta, take Elcy back to the ship." Any kindness I had witnessed from the captain before was non-existent.

"And let you have all the fun?" Quinta whined, her feathers ruffling.

"Now." The growl that came out of Captain Weyland's mouth went straight to my core.

Quinta rolled her eyes. "You're no fun."

"You're right, he's no fun," Captain Irelina agreed, making Captain Weyland bristle. "I was hoping to get a taste of the pixie."

"Now, Quinta," Captain Weyland snapped.

The harpy spun me around and wrapped her arms around my waist, carefully avoiding my wings. She took off without a warning, making me scream. There was a time when heights didn't scare me as much, but knowing I couldn't catch myself if I fell stole any confidence I once had.

I clung to the sticky feathers of Quinta's wings. I kept my eyes shut until she landed and let go of me.

"Stay out of trouble while I finish off Irelina's crew still on this ship."

I grabbed the harpy's arm. "You're not going to help him?"

"Captain Weyland can take care of himself." Quinta took off into the air with impeccable precision. As tempting as it was to watch her in action, my eyes immediately returned to the enemy ship, searching for the captain we left behind.

Screams and shouts filled my ears, and I dug my nails into the railing, chipping the designs. Giant waves raised in the sea around the enemy ship. I had never seen waves of that height and size, and it made my legs wobble. The water crashed down in a thunderous torrent. The ship split in two, exploding in a mass of splinters. I ducked as shards of wood flew my way. Cuts stung my arm from where I was protecting my head.

Silence replaced the cacophony as all eyes turned towards the explosion. I slowly stood, searching the planks of wood in the sea where a ship had been a moment before. Several bodies floated in the water, not all of them in one piece. I searched for the dark hair with a stripe of white in it, and every second that passed without my eyes on him made it impossible to breathe.

Soft footsteps echoed behind me. I spun, expecting Captain Weyland, even though he always made his presence known with clunky steps. Reamann approached with Aukina in tow. She had a wool blanket wrapped around her. The mermaid's hair was drenched, and she was void of clothes.

"I have never seen magic like that," Reamann said, unable to take his eyes off the wreckage.

"Captain Weyland was on the ship when it exploded." I gripped the railing harder to stop my body from shaking. It was nearly impossible to imagine anyone surviving an explosion like that, but he was a demon, a powerful one if the rumors were true. Surely that wouldn't have been enough to kill him.

Aukina passed her blanket to Reamann. "I'm going in." Before Reamann could comment, she dove off the side of the ship. Reamann rushed to the railing, just in time to see her head emerge from the water. The mermaid's long black hair fell from its braid and covered her shoulders. She flipped through the water, showing off her iridescent scales. She went from body to body, looking for the captain.

Crew members approached to watch the mermaid glide through the sea in search of their captain. It was a beautiful sight, but I couldn't appreciate it while I waited for her to find Captain Weyland's body. He risked his life to save me, and for what? So I could help retrieve an artifact that was supposed to save a kingdom. I didn't even know what the artifact did or how it would help.

The silence was suffocating. No one breathed as we waited for news.

"What is everyone staring at? We have work to do." The deep voice came from behind us, and it soothed my nerves.

Crew members scattered, revealing Captain Weyland. He was drenched, and his hat was nowhere to be seen, revealing the horns above his forehead. They glinted in the sunlight, almost looking dark red instead of black. He was back to the form I had become familiar with, a drenched version. A puddle of water formed beneath him, and his jaw was hard set.

I didn't think as I rushed forward, throwing my arms around the captain's waist. He was freezing from his wet clothes, but I didn't care.

"You're okay," I breathed.

"Were you worried, Sunshine?" His voice was low and deep in my ear, doing dangerous things to my body.

I pulled back, but I couldn't bring myself to let go of him. "I saw the ship explode."

His lips pulled into a crooked smile. "I'm the king of the sea, remember? I created those waves to destroy those stupid enough to touch you."

"I just thought..." My lip wobbled, and I had to cut myself off.

Captain Weyland cupped my cheek. "It'll take a lot more than that to kill a demon of my caliber."

I took a shaky breath. "What about Captain Irelina?"

Captain Weyland's jaw clenched. "She escaped."

"Did you say Irelina?" Aukina asked.

I pulled away from the captain, suddenly aware of the other eyes on us. Reamann held Aukina close to his side, her hair newly drenched. She held the captain's hat in her hand.

"What of it?" Captain Weyland asked.

Aukina pulled the blanket tighter around her body. "Irelina is the mermaid princess of the Calamity sea. Her family is known for being powerful and vicious. I was once engaged to her brother, but I heard she is worse than him."

"I know exactly who Irelina is," Captain Weyland grunted.

"Then you know that she won't stop until she gets what she wants, and if Elcy is what she wants..." Aukina's voice trailed off, and all eyes shifted to me.

My skin pricked, feeling like I was in more danger than before, but nothing had changed. I was warned this quest was going to be dangerous, and I wasn't about to ask to go home. We had come too far for that.

"Then we'll have to be prepared if she decides to come back." I smiled, ignoring the weight in my heart. "We shouldn't worry about what ifs, not when we won this battle." I glanced at the damaged ship, knowing it would slow us down, but I refused to get discouraged. "I think we should celebrate that win."

Reamann beamed at the suggestion. "I like the way you think."

"A good party would be nice to ease the tension," Aukina said. "I can even make snacks."

I turned to Captain Weyland, hoping for the same enthusiasm, but a cloud hung around him. "As long as the ship is fixed, do what you want," he snapped. He left without another word, and my stomach twisted. I didn't understand why he was upset.

When I looked at Reamann, he smirked, unfazed by the captain's mood. "Looks like we get to break out the drinks."

Chapter 15

It took three full days to repair the ship, which was an incredible speed. The promise of booze and a party kept the crew working all hours of the day and even part of the night. I did what I could to pick up debris, refusing to stand around while others did hard work, especially while knowing we were only attacked because of me.

Reamann helped others with the heavy lifting, while magic users did the majority of the repair work. They sealed and patched holes, and by the time they were done, the ship looked better than before the attack. It was incredible to see the crew work together, even with a death toll hanging over their heads. Five died during the fight. I hadn't known them, but it didn't stop me from feeling for them.

By the time the sky darkened on the last day of repairs, spirits lifted as the booze was lugged from below deck in large barrels and bottles. Several fires were lit in metal barrels around the deck, some with magic, some with regular wood. I found myself wrapped in a blanket next to Aukina and Reamann. Four others joined our group, including Quinta, Alre, a goblin, and a lesser demon. Alre passed drinks around, and when I took my first sip, I cringed.

"What is this?" My throat burned.

"Only the finest moonshine made on this ship." Alre tossed his glass back like it was nothing.

"Are there competitor moonshine makers on this ship?" Reamann took a swig of the booze. If it bothered him, he didn't show it.

"When you are stuck at sea for months at a time, we need something to entertain ourselves. Nights like tonight aren't uncommon, and we have a little competition to see who makes the best moonshine. This one burns in just the right way." Alre poured himself another drink.

"It hasn't killed me yet. That's what's important." Quinta tossed her own drink back.

I took another sip to try to match their pace, but I had never had something that hurt as it rolled down my throat. I preferred wines that tasted sweet compared to the moonshine. I could barely push a single swallow down my throat. Aukina seemed to be struggling the same as me.

"This has killed someone before?" Aukina looked at her glass wearily.

Quinta shrugged. "That's what you get when lazy goblins think they can do better than magically inclined fae."

"Watch it," the goblin next to her growled.

Quinta shrugged. "Am I wrong?" The goblin grumbled, refusing to answer.

Feeling uncomfortable at the exchange, I looked around, unsure of what I was searching for. Most crew members had settled around fires or went below deck to celebrate. A group played fiddles and drums in the center of the ship, and there were others dancing to the beat. It looked like fun, but I didn't want to go over there alone—not when I didn't know anyone dancing.

"The captain isn't here," Quinta said.

I tried to hide my surprise. "I wasn't looking for him."

She smirked as if she knew a secret I didn't. "He never joins us for these parties. He says it's because parties are beneath him, but I think it's because he knows his presence would kill the mood."

"He never joins?" I asked. My chest tightened at the thought. After days of not seeing him, I had hoped he'd join for the celebration.

"Never, but it's not because he's trying to preserve the mood," Alre said. "It's because he knows most of the crew is beneath him." Alre poured another drink down his throat, this time directly from the bottle.

"He can't possibly think that," I said. Captain Weyland seemed like a caring demon. He wouldn't have promised to get me to fly again otherwise.

"Don't mistake those lessons for kindness, darling," Alre said. "He needs you at your full potential. There's nothing more to it."

I clenched my fists, hating the way the quartermaster talked about the captain. "He's helping me out of kindness. He wouldn't use me like that."

"He's a pirate and demon. Of course, he would use you like that. Don't forget where you are. Pirates play by their own rules and moral codes, demons even more so. Let your guard down, and he'll take every advantage of you." The fire danced in Alre's eyes. His words felt foreboding, but I didn't like them. Weyland had saved me multiple times. Yes, he needed me to retrieve the artifact, but it was more than that. I could tell.

"Don't listen to him," Quinta said. "He just has a stick up his ass ever since the captain scolded him for sending you up to the crow's nest."

Alre took another swig. "How was I supposed to know a pixie was too scared to fly?"

Quinta snatched the bottle from him, throwing back the rest of the liquid in it. "Don't listen to him," she repeated.

"I'm your superior. I could have you thrown off the ship for insubordination." Alre grabbed a bottle from the goblin next to him. The goblin grumbled while keeping his voice low. He grabbed his buddy and sauntered off, deciding that the quartermaster was no longer good company.

Quinta laughed. "Without me, this ship would get lost at sea. No one can chart the stars like me, and you all wouldn't be able to tell your heads from your asses." She tried to take the new bottle from Alre, but he was prepared for her and easily dodged the attack.

"You're the navigator?" I asked. With the way the harpy had fought during the battle, I had assumed she was a warrior.

"Only the best in the great seas." She winked at me as she laced her fingers behind her head and propped her feet up on the edge of the barrel, not concerned about the flames dancing inches away from her feet.

"Mermaids rely on a combination of the stars and currents to know where they are," Aukina said. "It's not an easy skill to learn."

"I used to study the stars when I lived with my flock, and I've read about star charting, but I've never had a need for it. Living in the same place for nearly my entire life limits the need to navigate the world." There were many nights before Ethlow when I would lie on a blanket and look up at the stars as I waited for sleep to take me.

Since arriving at Ethlow, I hadn't seen the stars, since it was too dangerous to leave the estate at night. As I looked up at the sky, it was covered in glittering lights that brought me back to the past. In the grand scheme of things, I was just a speck in the world. It often made me feel like I didn't matter. That feeling was what kept me stuck at Ethlow for decades, but I wasn't sure if I could go back to the same life as before.

I took a long drink, finishing what had been poured for me. The burn was a good distraction from my own thoughts.

"If you want, I can show you a little about star charting," Quinta said.

I looked away from the sky and found the harpy studying me. "Really?"

She shrugged. "I think everyone should have basic knowledge of where they are. How else will they know where they're going?"

"By using an arrogant harpy to chart the way," Alre muttered.

Quinta laughed. "Come on. Let's go dance and leave this grumpy ass to wallow in his misery."

The navigator grabbed Aukina's and my hands and dragged us towards the center of the deck. Reamann followed like a lost puppy. Once we were on the makeshift dance floor, the beat of the drums made my blood pulse. Or maybe it was the alcohol coursing through my system. My head grew fuzzy, but I didn't care as I swung my hips to the rhythm, letting myself get lost in the celebration. Another cup of moonshine was shoved into my hand, but it didn't taste as bad as the first one. Or maybe that was my taste buds going numb.

I danced with Aukina and Quinta at separate times and together. I didn't want to stop moving, needing to burn off the swirling energy in my system. The more I laughed, the more pixie dust shimmered off my wing, and the bigger the crowd watching us grew.

"Show us what you can do with that glitter!" someone from the crowd shouted.

Whenever my pixie dust got out of control, I did what I could to rein it in, but my usual defenses were gone, and nothing was holding me back. For a moment, I wasn't a prisoner in my own head.

I scooped pixie dust into my hands and watched it glow like a million stars. I blew gently, and the specks floated into the air, spinning into different shapes, starting with hearts before molding into more complex designs, the most intricate being a female dressed in the leathers of a warrior. She pulled back a glittering bow, and when she released it, the arrow flew over the heads of the crowds and exploded into stardust.

I giggled as the crowd cooed at the sight. It was a simple trick I used to do for the pixies in my flock. It had made children laugh and stopped their tears. It entertained the elderly, who had more magic than me, but few bothered to learn the act. To me, it was like painting the sky in the most beautiful way.

I hadn't tried it since going to Ethlow, afraid I had lost that skill along with the ability to fly.

"Make a mermaid!" Aukina clapped her hands together, glee filling her face.

I flicked my hand and swooped my fingers, creating the image of a mermaid swimming through the sea. More requests were flung at me, and I easily obliged, loving the attention.

"Again!" another shout echoed in my ear.

I stepped to do another, but I stumbled forward. I caught myself, but my legs were unsteady. I started another trick, but a gentle hand grabbed my arm.

"I think it's time the two of you get to bed before you hurt yourselves," Reamann said.

I blinked twice before realizing he was also holding onto Aukina, who was giggling. Her laughter made my own explode. The guardsman pulled us away from the crowd, earning him a chorus of complaints. With a single look, the crowd backed up. Reamann looked like a puppy dog during the day, but when the night came, his skin turned to coal and horns sprouted from his head.

"Hey, Reamann, why do you only look like a demon at night?" I had been wondering this since he first shifted into his demon form, but I had stopped myself from asking, knowing it was rude. I couldn't remember why I thought that. It seemed harmless now.

"Because he's a half-demon," Aukina said. "He doesn't have as much control over his form like some demons, but it makes for a fun night. Did you know in demon form he has two dicks?" Aukina giggled as Reamann's eyes bulged out of his head.

"I don't think Elcy wants to hear about that," Reamann grumbled.

Reamann was far from wrong with that statement. My interest shot into the sky like a shooting star. "Two dicks? How does that work? Do they both go in one hole?"

"Sometimes, but I think it's more fun to utilize different holes." The mermaid wiggled her brows, and the demon rolled his eyes.

"Aukina!" Reamann shook his head. "I definitely need to get you to bed."

"I'm not ready to sleep," Aukina whined. She clung to Reamann's arms, pressing her plush chest against the demon.

The demon's body stiffened. He looked at me, and his face tightened like he was in pain. "Are you okay to get back to your cabin on your own?"

I let go of Reamann as I bit back my laugh. "I'm older than both of you combined. I don't need assistance from you."

That was all the reassurance Reamann needed. He let go of me and scooped Aukina into his arms. He practically ran to their room, and I couldn't stop smiling. I wasn't sure if I had ever witnessed two beings more in love than them. I loved it, but my chest tightened just a little. I had dreamed about love since I was a little girl. Over the past century, I had dated a few males here and there, but none of the relationships were what I wanted. It had always felt like something was missing.

I looked up at the sky. The hole in my heart widened as I wondered if I'd ever find the kind of love and adventure I had craved. After a century of being alive, that hope dwindled to an ember on the verge of flickering out of existence. There were many beings who only got a fraction of that kind of time, and they found more passion and love than all of my relationships combined. I didn't understand how they had done it.

"Hey there, beautiful."

I looked around, suddenly aware that I was standing on the deck and staring at the sky like a fool. A tall elf stood only a few feet away. He was part of the crew that worked the cannons, but I didn't know his name.

"Oh, hi." I smiled, unsure of what else to do.

"I saw those tricks you were doing earlier, and I'm impressed. I don't think I've ever seen a pixie before, and I had no idea they could do something like that." The firelight flickered against his tanned skin, showing off his muscles. He should've been wearing a coat with the cold air.

"You've never seen a pixie before?" I asked. Most pixie flocks stayed in the kingdom of Lyranta, but I was sure there were flocks that had wandered into other kingdoms.

"Before you came along, I thought they were extinct. That's why Captain Irelina was desperate to get her hands on you."

I took a breath, trying to process that information, but with the amount of alcohol in my system, it felt like swimming through fog.

"But I think you are incredible. I was hoping you'd be willing to give me a private show," the elf said. He smiled sweetly, making me feel safe.

I looked around as I debated. Reamann had said I needed to go to bed, but I didn't feel tired, and he and Aukina ran off to do the opposite of sleeping. "Okay," I agreed, seeing no reason not to.

The elf grabbed my hand and led me to part of the deck that was away from the fire. It was colder there, but I was sure he wanted the darkness to see better.

As we reached a corner hidden by the wall of the rooms on the first floor of the ship, the elf spun me around until my back hit the wall. He pressed his hand next to my head, trapping me between his body and the wood behind me.

"I thought you wanted a show." My heart pounded as an uneasy feeling filled my chest.

He leaned in, brushing his lips against my ear. "I do. I want to see what else that luscious body of yours can do." His hand ran down my side until it settled between my thighs. I squirmed, trying to get away from him, but I was trapped.

"What are you doing?" I pushed at his chest, but he didn't budge.

"You know, when I touch a female here, usually she spreads her legs for me."

My body shook at the implication. I shoved harder against his chest, but it was like pushing against stone. "Stop. I don't want to do anything like that with you."

"Oh, come on. I know you are dying to be touched by someone. I promise I can make you feel good, baby."

"No!" I pushed again, but it felt futile. My chest was on the verge of collapsing. I didn't understand what was going on, and my skin prickled.

"What the fuck do you think you're doing touching my treasure?"

Chapter 16

The elf froze as Captain Weyland's voice boomed like thunder. My heart ran rampant, both terrified and relieved.

"Captain, what are you doing here? I didn't think you'd join the party." The elf pulled back just enough to look at Captain Weyland, but he didn't remove his hand from between my legs.

Captain Weyland stalked forward and grabbed the elf's arm. He ripped it away from my body before twisting it. A loud snap rang out from the elf's body, and he cried out in pain. "You dare to touch my treasure and think you had the right to question me?" The air thickened with the demon's power.

The elf quivered, but he didn't have the intelligence to keep his mouth shut. "She's not yours. We were just going to have a little fun. She agreed to it."

Captain Weyland twisted his arm, causing another pop and scream. "I distinctly heard her telling you no." The demon dragged the elf to the edge of the ship and held his hand against the railing. With his freehand, he pulled out a dagger and held it over the elf's arm. "I should cut off your hand for touching her inappropriately."

The male whimpered, and his pants grew dark with liquid. "Please. No. I need my hand." Tears streamed down the elf's face as he begged the captain.

The captain's silver eyes darkened, nearly turning black as the air thickened around him. Tall waves crashed into the ship, making it rock back and forth.

"Give me one good reason not to." Captain Weyland was steady on his feet, despite the undulating ship.

"I'm one of your best gunners."

"Not good enough."

"You need me on Dragon's Breath Island."

"There are plenty of other elves I can use."

Captain Weyland didn't give him another chance to answer. He swung the blade down, cutting clean through the elf's wrist. The gunner screamed, and his legs gave out, but the captain didn't release him, even as blood sprayed. "Touch her again, and I'll cut off more than just your hand. Do you understand?"

A mangled cry escaped the elf's mouth as he stared at the space his hand once was. It wasn't enough for the captain.

"Do. You. Understand?" His voice was icier than the dead of winter.

"Yes!" the male cried.

Captain Weyland released the crew member and took a step back. "Good. Now get out of here before I change my mind and cut more off now."

The elf cradled his hand against his chest and took off in a staggered run. The captain watched him until he was out of sight.

Only then did he flip the dagger back into the sheath on his belt. He turned to me, taking his time to look me up and down.

"Are you hurt?"

"You cut off his hand," I stuttered as I stared at the blood staining the floor.

The captain moved towards me, leaving little space between us. I should have been afraid of him, especially after what I had witnessed, but the captain's warmth was strangely comforting. He cupped my cheek and stroked my face with his thumb. The gesture was gentle, and it made tears spill out of my eyes.

"I should have killed him for touching you." Weyland pressed his hand above my head and closed his eyes. The next breath he took was shaky as he struggled to control his body.

"You didn't need to go that far."

Captain Weyland took my chin and forced me to look at him. "You said no, and he didn't listen. I don't put up with males who think they can do whatever they want to a female, and now he'll think twice about touching someone without permission again. I may cross a lot of lines, but that is never one I will allow to happen on my ship."

My throat was dry as the captain's words settled in. When the elf touched me, fear had crept through my veins, terrified of how far he would have pushed. Captain Weyland stopped that from happening. It was more violent than I would have handled it, but I couldn't deny that he saved me. Again.

"Now, tell me, Sunshine. Are you okay?"

I nodded slowly, unsure if I was. My head spun, but with the captain only inches away, it felt as if he'd destroy the world if that was what it took to keep me safe.

"I want to hear you say it." His eyes held mine captive, his irises dancing as he waited for my answer.

"I'm okay." My lip trembled, even though I meant the words. My head spun from the evening, and a wave of exhaustion filled my body. "I should go back to my room and get some sleep."

"You're not going anywhere, Sunshine." The captain leaned in like he was going to kiss me. I closed my eyes in anticipation, but only the cool breeze touched my lips. The lack of heat made my eyes flutter open. The captain's chest heaved with slow, steady breaths.

His anger simmered, but I couldn't tell if it was directed towards me. It made my heart race at the thought.

"Are you okay?" It felt like a foolish question to ask a demon who had just cut off another male's hand.

Captain Weyland let out a sharp laugh. "You're asking me if I'm okay when you were the one assaulted?"

"If I upset you in some way—"

"No, I'm not okay. All evening, I've been trying to stay away from the party, away from you, because I didn't know if I could control myself. When I finally give in and come find you, what do I find? That grimy little elf with his hands all over you. I should have killed him." He clenched his jaw and hit his fist above my head.

I flinched out of reflex, but I wasn't scared. Maybe it was foolish, but I placed my hand on the demon's chest. His eyes flicked down at the contact, and his pupils flared. "You protected me from him, and that's more than enough."

"I should start a tally of how many times I save you, because that number is growing exponentially." Weyland's demon powers settled as we slipped back into our banter, but his body was rigid, as if he was waiting to destroy the next thing that touched me.

"I should learn to defend myself, so I don't keep ending up as the damsel." I had never felt as helpless as I had since stepping on Captain Weyland's ship. "I'm sure you're tired of saving me." A weight pressed against my chest. If I couldn't protect myself, how did I expect to protect anyone else?

His thumb brushed over my bottom lip. "I will always protect you, Elcy."

My name on his tongue sent a shiver down my spine. My chest swelled with warmth as I thought about everything he had done for me. He was the dreaded pirate Captain Weyland, and I understood better than ever that the title was accurate and fitting. But what all the rumors left out was the kindness in his heart. Even if he did things that most would consider morally wrong, he did it with good intentions. He was a good male.

I lifted onto my toes, but I stopped just before our lips met. "Kiss me."

He leaned in, stopping himself before our lips met. His eyes burned with desire, but he didn't close the space between us. "You've been drinking."

"I don't care." Maybe that was the alcohol burning in my system, or maybe it was the adrenaline from the demon saving me, but

I was tired of holding back. Even if it brought me heartache, I wanted the demon for the night.

"You're going to regret this." Before I could back out, he brought his lips to mine with a surprising gentleness. Our mouths moved as if we were both afraid the moment wasn't real. His hand tangled in my hair, and he deepened the kiss. As his tongue swiped against my mouth, asking for entrance, I knew I was done for. I wrapped my arms around his neck and parted my lips. The fuzziness from the alcohol disappeared, and my mind felt sharp and clear as Weyland slid his tongue into my mouth.

In almost every way, I was confused by what was happening, but what I did know was that I wanted more. I wanted the pirate's rough hands roaming my body, replacing the touch of every male that came before him. His fingers dug into my lower back, pulling me flushed against him. His other hand slid from my hair and down my neck, sending tingles crawling over my skin. The moan that escaped my mouth was involuntary.

Weyland pulled back much too soon. "We can't do this here." He was as breathless as I felt.

A wave of disappointment and horror crashed over me. Crossing lines with the captain was a dangerous game to play. It was best to walk away before things went further, but I couldn't bring my feet to move. Not when the taste of his lips lingered on mine.

"Maybe we shouldn't do this at all," I whispered, a fraction of my senses returning.

"Tell me to stop, and I will." His breath was heavy as he struggled to control himself, but after what he did to his own crew member for touching me, I knew one word would end this.

"Don't stop," I whispered. The need burning in my core was too much to ignore. It was stupid and naïve to crawl into bed with a demon pirate, but for a moment, I stopped thinking with my head and let go.

Weyland kissed me again. This time his hands roamed my body, taking his time to touch my every curve. When his hand found my ass, he squeezed, making me squeak. A guttural noise erupted from his chest.

"If we don't move this somewhere private, I might lose it. I don't want anyone else hearing the noises I plan on making come out of you, because I might kill anyone who hears the noises meant only for me." His thumb brushed over my bottom lip.

"Who says this mouth is only for you?" I asked, holding my chin defiantly. It was the worst kind of lie, especially as the throbbing between my legs made my core slick with desire.

"Because you're mine, Sunshine."

Chapter 17

Weyland wrapped his arms around my waist and threw me over his shoulder. I gasped at the sudden motion. He moved with purpose towards his office.

He kicked the door open, slamming it shut once we were inside. With a flick of his hand, the door locked. He was already moving to his room, locking that door, too. He tossed me onto the bed, and I was painfully aware of every part of my body that jiggled.

I looked up at the pirate, waiting for disgust to fill his eyes at the sight, but I found something entirely unexpected. He rubbed his jaw as he looked down at me, hunger burning brightly. "I can't decide how I want to take you, Sunshine, so I'm going to let you choose. Do you want it hard and fast until you see stars, or do you want me to take my time savoring every inch of that gorgeous body of yours?"

I lost my breath. Both suggestions warmed my thighs. I should've told him to stop. I should've gone back to my room before I crossed the line I couldn't come back from, but I knew deep down it wasn't what I wanted in my heart. It made no sense to fall for the vicious pirate captain, but every time he called me

Sunshine, every time he saved me from imminent danger, another piece of me fell for him.

"Slow," I whispered. There was a part of me that wanted to see the captain unleash himself as he ravaged me, but not for the first time. I had never had a one-night-stand before. I wasn't that kind of girl. My heart was tied to my body, and I knew once I gave the demon pirate permission to ravage me, he'd take every piece of my heart. It was a stupid decision, but I was tired of worrying about consequences.

Weyland smirked. He pulled at the string tying the top of his shirt together. It fell open in a V, revealing his toned pecs and the intricate chain tattoos beneath. The design wasn't anything like I had seen before. I shifted onto my knees to get a better look. He stripped his shirt off and tossed it to the side. My fingers reached up on their own and traced the black lines etched into his skin. The chains criss-crossed between his pecs before wrapping around his arms.

A deep groan rumbled from his chest. "If you keep doing that, I won't be able to savor this."

"Oh?" I looked up at him, widening my eyes to make myself look as innocent as possible. I couldn't bring myself to stop as I ran my fingers lower, tracing the ridges of his body. When I reached his pants, he grabbed both of my wrists.

He brought my wrist to his mouth and peppered soft kisses down my arm. When he reached my elbow, he pulled back. His fingers found the hem of my shirt, and he pulled it off. His eyes scanned my bare torso, and I held my breath, afraid of his response.

Weyland knelt on the ground in front of me. With his height, it made it so we were at eye level. His hands rested on my hips, but he didn't move to remove my bottoms. "I need to taste you." The strain in his voice showed he was struggling to hold back.

I blinked once, waiting for him to make good on his words. Then I realized he was waiting for me to give him permission. It only made me want him more.

I grabbed the back of his head and pulled him into a kiss. I parted just enough to whisper, "Please."

That was the only word he needed. He tore my bottoms off, leaving me completely exposed. The pirate hooked his arms under my thighs and pulled me to the edge of the bed, making me lose balance and fall back onto the mattress. He kept my thighs on his shoulders as he used his fingers to open me up for him. He ran his tongue through my folds, the sensation making me jolt.

I couldn't remember the last time someone had their mouth between my legs, especially one who knew how to use his tongue like Weyland. He stroked up and down, swirling around my clit. My back arched as he flicked his wet muscle in a swift motion. The pirate grabbed my hips and pinned me down, refusing to let me squirm as he coaxed pleasure from my body.

My head spun, and my breath grew rapid, but I needed more to reach my climax. His tongue alone wasn't enough to bring me to that point, but it didn't stop him from taking his time enjoying every crevice.

"Captain Weyland," I moaned as my patience wore thin.

He pulled back and smirked. "I thought you said you wanted me to take my time."

"Not that much time," I whimpered. My body ached for his touch. I wanted him to fill me completely and make me feel alive.

Weyland crawled on top of me and pinned my hands above my head. He brushed his lips against my ears. "Don't call me captain. I want you to use my name." He nipped my ear, making me moan. "Now, ask me the right way, and I'll think about giving you what you want." He rolled his hips against mine, showing me exactly what was waiting for me beneath his pants.

"Weyland, I want you to fuck me." My voice dripped with desperation, but I didn't care. Not when I needed the demon pirate inside of me.

"That's a good girl." He pressed a kiss against my lips as if it was a reward. Then he reached for his pants, unbuckling them just enough to pull himself free.

The pirate stroked his cock through my folds. I looked down to see what I was getting myself into, but I couldn't see his size between the rolls on my stomach and the angle I was laying at. He took his time, making sure he was thoroughly covered in my arousal.

Weyland shifted, pushing my knees higher. He lined up at my entrance and pushed in slightly. I gasped at the sensation. It felt incredible, and I couldn't wait to know what it felt like to have him inside of me. He leaned forward, bringing his face back to mine. His gaze was intense as he watched me. My breath was shallow as I looked up at the pirate captain. I hadn't expected tonight to end with me in his bed. It felt like a wild dream, one like I used to wish for before I had become complacent.

He kissed me as he rolled his hips, pushing into me until he filled me completely. The motion was slow and gentle, the opposite of what I had expected from a demon. Weyland seemed like a pirate that did whatever he could to get what he wanted, and I was what he wanted.

He moved in and out slowly, and with each thrust, my body buzzed with pleasure. The way he moved was careful and caring, and my pixie dust poured off my wings as Weyland and I moved as one.

When I couldn't take it anymore, I grabbed his neck and pulled him closer. "Please. I need more."

He smirked at me, as if he had been waiting for me to beg for what I wanted. He grabbed my leg and hoisted it higher. It shifted the angle of his thrusts, making him hit a spot that lit my body on fire. The pirate leaned forward and took my nipple in his mouth, sucking and nipping as he massaged the other breast. The mix of all the sensations was too much, and my muscles tightened as the pressure built. My toes curled, and I cried out as an explosion erupted within me.

Weyland picked up his pace, making his thrusts sharp and fast as pleasure continued to course through me. With a final thrust, he spilled into me, groaning from his own pleasure. His chest heaved as he looked down at me, searching my face for something. Maybe signs of regret?

He brushed the hair out of my face and kissed my forehead. "You are even more beautiful when you're writhing beneath me."

His comment made my skin flush, which I knew was blatantly obvious. I licked my lips, unsure of what to say.

"Let's get you cleaned up," he said, making it so I didn't have to talk. He picked me up and carried me to the bath, keeping me upright, even as my eyes grew heavy. "Just rest, Sunshine. I'll take care of you."

Chapter
18

I woke up with a pounding headache. For a moment, I couldn't remember what had happened or where I was. The bed was too soft to be the one in my cabin. When I noticed the thick arm draped over my waist, it all came flooding back. Weyland stopping the elf before cutting off his hand. Him bringing me back to his room. The way he touched my body, making me feel things no other male had accomplished. Then there was the time he took to clean me up. He had been gentle and thorough, making sure I was okay after everything that had happened. No male had attempted that kind of care with me after sex.

I turned around to face the pirate captain. His hair fell around his horns in messy waves. Weyland was always so put together, and it was nice to see him with his walls down. It was also nice to wake up to his shirtless torso. I traced my fingers over his arms, tracing the chain tattoos, wondering what made him get that specific tattoo.

"What are you doing, Sunshine?" Weyland grumbled. His eyes cracked open, sleep heavy on his face.

"Just admiring you." I bit my lower lip at the admission.

"Careful. If you keep touching me like that, the morning is going to heat up fast." There was no room for argument in his tone.

His suggestion made it difficult to keep my hands to myself, because round two sounded delightful, but my head and body ached. I wanted to be properly rested when I experienced his glorious body again, because I knew one taste wasn't enough. I pulled my hand back, but Weyland captured it, bringing it to his lips. The soft kiss on the back of my knuckles made my heart flutter. Was that how it was supposed to feel when in a relationship with the right person?

"Where did your tattoos come from?" Before last night, I wouldn't have felt comfortable enough to ask the captain a personal question like that, but his legs were tangled in mine, making me feel connected to the male who had been inside of me hours prior.

"Where any tattoo comes from." His lazy smirk drove me wild.

I smacked his chest playfully. "That's not what I meant."

Weyland rolled over, pinning me beneath him. "Aren't you the one who loves words, so your intentions are clear?" He shifted his leg, pressing it between my thighs. The slight friction made it difficult to breathe.

"What made you compelled to ink chains on your body?" I asked, glaring at the demon's teasing.

"Maybe I'll show you sometime." His words were layered with hidden meaning, but as he pressed his lips against mine, it made it difficult to remember to ask him for clarification.

Weyland pulled back from the kiss, leaving me breathless. I wanted nothing more than to stay in bed with him all day, but that bubble popped quickly.

"We should start our training session for the day before the rest of the hungover crew wakes up," Weyland said. He pulled away and rolled to the edge of the bed, grabbing a clean shirt.

"We could always stay in bed all day. I don't think anyone will miss us." I bit my lower lip as I waited for his answer. My core throbbed from his touch, and I ached for more. It was as if a void had opened into a well of desire, and I couldn't stop thinking about the way it felt for the captain to be between my legs.

"That's tempting." His lips curled into a smirk. "Very tempting. But there's one problem."

"Problem?" My heart thundered, waiting for the bad news.

"You're not on any contraceptives, are you?"

My eyes widened as horror washed over me. I let the demon spill his seed into me without a thought. All it took was one time for an accident to happen. "No."

Weyland grunted. "That can't happen again until that changes. I'm not interested in having children."

My chest tightened at the admission. "Not ever?"

"Life on the sea is no life for a child," he said. He grabbed his hat from the nightstand and put it on his head. He pulled his coat on, making him look as put together as usual.

"But don't you ever want to settle down and have a family?" His response shouldn't have mattered. Having sex one time didn't mean we were committed to each other, but it felt like there was something more going on between us. He cared about me. I knew that, but I had always imagined settling down and having children one day.

"My heart belongs to the sea, and the sea never settles. That is the beauty of it."

It felt as if my heart was shattering as I realized last night had meant two very different things for me and the pirate.

"Maybe we shouldn't do that again. It'd be better to keep our relationship professional." I couldn't look at Weyland, not after what he said.

I felt his eyes on me, and the seconds he took to respond felt like minutes. "Do you regret last night?"

The answer should've been yes. I had known all along that climbing into bed with the captain would only end in heartbreak. I had done it anyway, believing there was a chance things would end differently.

"No," I said, and I meant it. I forced myself to get out of bed and put on my clothes. "It just can't happen again if there is no future between us."

"A pirate and a pixie don't belong together. It's just like sunshine and rain don't go together." Weyland's voice was tight, and his face was hard. If there was any doubt before, there weren't any now. Last night was only physical for the demon. It meant nothing to him.

"Under the right circumstances, sunshine and rain can create a rainbow, but clearly that's not the case for us." I slipped out of the room before he could see the tears in my eyes.

Days passed without a sighting of the captain. It was incredible how easy it was to avoid someone on a ship. I had expected to run into Weyland everywhere I went. My eyes scanned the deck every time I stepped onto it, and when the demon was nowhere to be seen, my heart sank a little more.

It was stupid. He made his intentions clear, but part of me had hoped he was just too scared to admit his real feelings. His lack of presence said more than his words did. He was avoiding me after my rejection.

I leaned against the railing of the ship, resting my chin on my arms. The waves were as non-existent as the wind, but it didn't stop the ocean from parting for the ship. It was easy to zone out while watching it.

Flapping wings pulled me out of my thoughts. Quinta lowered herself onto the railing next to me. She plopped onto her butt with her back to the ocean. Her talons dug into the wood, keeping her balanced.

"What's got you so down, pixie?" She kicked her legs as she tilted her head.

I smiled as a reaction, not realizing my thoughts were written on my face. "It's nothing."

"I don't believe you. You have been smiling ever since you stepped onto this ship—until after the party. You've had a cloud around your head for days now." She leaned in, bringing her face close to mine. "Let me guess. It has something to do with a male."

"How did you know?" Weyland didn't seem like the type to brag about his conquests to his crew, and I didn't think anyone had seen us.

"Elmon has been going off about the captain being insane and not fit for leading this crew. He even tried to start a coup." A sharp laugh escaped her mouth. "Like anyone would follow that assface over the captain, especially after learning what happened. From what I gather, the newly one-handed elf tried to touch you inappropriately, and the captain took his hand for it." Quinta looked down at her claws. "Elmon should count himself lucky. I would have cut off his dick before tearing out his bowels and leaving him to bleed to death if I had been the one to find him. I still might do that if he doesn't shut up about it."

I pinched my lips together, unsure of how to respond. I wasn't used to the level of violence on the pirate ship, but it didn't feel like my place to say anything.

"It's not Elmon who's bringing me down." I hadn't thought about that incident since it happened. Weyland stopped him before anything had happened, and my mind had been too consumed with the captain to think about much else.

"So it's the captain then. I had a feeling."

"You did?"

Quinta chuckled. "It's not hard to see that you like him. You get hearts in your eyes every time you see him, but he's been keeping to himself for the past few days, right about the same time your mood dropped."

I chewed on my inner cheek as I stared at the calm ocean. "Am I that obvious?"

"It couldn't be more obvious if you had it written in big red letters on your forehead." The harpy cackled at her own comment. "But it's not worth going down that road. He's not the type to settle down, and you are. You two belong in different worlds."

My shoulders deflated. "I'm starting to realize that." I didn't want to admit it. If two people were meant to be, then they could get through anything. I wanted to believe Weyland was the one I had been waiting for. The feelings that burned for him were new to me. They ran deeper than I thought possible, which made no sense. When I thought back on all our interactions, I barely knew the captain. It was best to move on and not worry about it.

"I'd usually suggest you get over your feelings by getting under someone else, but I don't think that's smart in this case. The captain can be a bit possessive, and after Elmon, I don't want to know what he'd do if he found out you shared a bed with another." Quinta's eyes glinted, making me doubt that statement was true. It was as if she craved violence and wanted to see exactly what the captain would do.

"Why would he care if I slept with someone else when it's not like we're together?" My chest tightened as I thought back on our conversation. Weyland was the one that said there was no future for us.

"Because knowing you're no good for someone is different than falling for that same someone. I'm sure you know that better than anyone." She winked before using her wings to jump to her feet, carefully balancing on the railing. "Come find me on the quarter-deck after dark, and I'll teach you about star charting. That'll get your mind off the captain." She took off into the air, moving with incredible grace. There was a time I had been able to move like that, but I didn't know if it'd ever happen again. With Weyland avoiding me, our flying training had ceased—not that our lessons had been yielding results.

Chapter 19

I waited for darkness to consume the night sky before venturing to the quarterdeck. Quinta stood over the wheel, gently correcting its position.

"Good evening," I said.

Quinta looked up, and a smile crawled onto her face. "You came."

"You invited me. Why wouldn't I?"

"That kind of logic could get you in trouble." Quinta stepped away from the wheel.

I was grateful for the dark, so my blush wasn't as obvious. It had already gotten me in trouble with that elf, but I wasn't about to say that. "So, where are the star charts?" I looked around for the maps and charts I had expected to be splayed on the deck.

Quinta laughed. "Oh no. That's too complicated for lesson one. Charts take years to learn and properly use. Today, we are going to teach you to find your way home."

"You can do that without charts?"

Quinta waved me over. "It's pretty simple. There are five major stars in the sky, one for each of the elements: wind, water, fire, earth, and magic. They are the brightest stars in the sky, so they are easy to find." I nodded along, remembering reading about the major constellations.

"Phoenix Rising marks the east. It's easy to tell, because it has three smaller stars, which look like its tail." Quinta gestured to the sky, guiding my eyes toward the constellation. "That one over there is Frozen Gate. If you look at the surrounding stars, it looks like a snowflake. That's the northern star. This one over here is the Dragon's Wing. I don't think I need to explain why that one looks like that. That's the southern star. To the west, we have the Mountain's Grief. It's supposed to look like a crumbling mountain, but I've never been able to see why. Finally, we have the most important star: The Mystic Sigil. It looks like a giant spiral, and at the center is the brightest star in the night sky. If you know where that star is when you are home, then you can follow it back to where you came from."

I had read about star constellations and how navigators used them to chart their way, but it was different listening to Quinta explain it. "That seems so simple."

"In a way, it is, but there is more to it. The pattern of the stars changes with the season, and if you get off course during the day, you may not know until the stars come out again. Then there's the weather to contend with. When it's cloudy for weeks on end, you have to find other ways to navigate the seas."

I nodded, understanding that a simple explanation of something didn't make the practice simple.

"So, how would I find my way home from here?" I couldn't tear my eyes away from the stars. There was something about seeing them on the sea that made them magical. When the water was calm, the light from the stars reflected against the dark water.

"It's pretty easy. The Mystic Sigil lies in the center of the mainland, but Kinzlea is to the east, so you would follow the Mystic Sigil until it's centered and then move towards Phoenix Rising. The most important thing with star charting is to understand where you're coming from, where you are, and where you're going. Once you get that down, it's all in the nuances."

I nodded, committing her words to memory. If I ever wanted to break free from Ethlow and explore the world, then I would need to learn to navigate it.

Heavy footsteps alerted us to the incoming presence. Without seeing who climbed those steps, I already knew who it was. There was only one demon on this ship that held that kind of presence.

Weyland looked at Quinta, not bothering to acknowledge my presence. "How are we fairing on time?"

Quinta stood straighter in the presence of the captain. "We are ahead of schedule, even with the slight delay from Irelina. I'd say we have a week if we don't run into any storms along the way."

The captain nodded. "Let's hope we don't run into any storms, then."

"Is that all? I'd like to get back to my lesson with Elcy."

"No. I'd like to talk to the pixie in private," Weyland said. He hadn't looked at me yet, even as my eyes burned into him, desperate for any kind of acknowledgement.

I had it bad, and I didn't know what to do. I couldn't make Weyland want a life with me, but I couldn't get my heart to let go of the pirate.

"She's all yours." Quinta took off, leaving me alone with the captain. Only then did he acknowledge my presence.

"Did you need something?" I swallowed hard, trying to keep my mind professional.

"We will continue our flying lessons tomorrow. I have also asked Alre to teach you self-defense. Once we reach the island, that's where the real danger is, and I may not be available to swoop in and save you." His tone was flat, and he barely looked at me.

I ignored the ache in my chest. I didn't come on the adventure to find love. I came to help King Zathrian, so everyone at Ethlow could stay safe. "I can ask Reamann to teach me. I'm sure the quartermaster has better things to do than deal with me."

"No." His voice was hard. "Reamann is a skilled fighter, but he's too nice. You don't need someone to praise you for doing something wrong. You need to be able to fight on your own."

"That's not going to happen in a week." I had attended the weekly defense classes Reamann taught at Ethlow for months, and I felt no more skilled than before. I had been helpless with Elmon.

"You'd be surprised what Alre can accomplish."

I rolled my eyes at the commands. Weyland spent days avoiding me, and now he thought he could give me orders. "I'll think about it."

I walked away from him towards the back of the ship. I grabbed the railing, hoping the captain would leave. Breathing the same air as him was harder than I had anticipated. I wanted to yell at him and kiss him at the same time. Neither of those things were options.

"This isn't a game, Sunshine." Weyland stood behind me, making the hair on my neck raise. I was painfully aware of the distance between us.

"I know that. I know what's at stake, but no one has even told me what my role is in all of this. Instead of training me to fight—something I'll never be able to do—maybe you should tell me what the hell I'm supposed to do to retrieve this artifact—another thing no one has bothered to tell me about." It had been easy to not worry about that when I had other things on my mind, but knowing we were only a week away from our destination reminded me why I was on the stupid pirate ship.

"What do you want to know?" Weyland moved next to me, pressing his forearms against the railing. There was barely space between our arms, making me want to close the distance between us.

"Tell me why you need a pixie to retrieve this artifact. What is it about my magic that differs from yours, fae magic, or elven magic?" I should have asked that much sooner, but I was told I was needed, and I accepted that. It was different now that time was ticking. In a matter of a week, I was expected to retrieve the artifact, but I didn't know how that was supposed to happen.

Weyland reached back and let the pixie dust fall into his scooped hand. He brought it in front of us, cradling it like it was precious. "Many think that all magic is the same, but it's far from that.

Demons get their power from the underworld. Elves get their magic from nature. Fae get their magic from their gods. But pixies... They get their magic from the sun. Many think pixies and demons are destined to be mortal enemies.

"Afraid of demons, pixies, elves, and fae banded together to protect this artifact. They used all three types of magic, but the pixies were the most involved. We need a pixie, an elf, and a fae to get through the wards, and as I know, you're the only pixie left in the mortal realm." He let the pixie dust fall from his fingers. The wind swept it away.

My spine snapped straight. "What do you mean?" Elmon had made a comment about pixie's being rare, but I hadn't thought much of it. It made sense that a pirate wouldn't see many beings who liked to stay hidden in the forest.

Weyland looked at me, sorrow weighing down his face. "I thought you knew. Twenty years ago, pixie flocks were hunted and slaughtered in an attempt to eliminate them. Without a pixie, the artifact would be lost to the world."

Blood pounded in my head. I knew my flock had been murdered, but I hadn't heard about the decimation of pixies. Living at Ethlow was like living in a bubble in the world. My whole body felt faint, and I gripped the railing until my knuckles turned white.

My throat tightened as I thought back to the night that changed my life. The night my entire flock was murdered. I had never understood why it had happened. We had never done anything to upset others. We kept to ourselves, and we helped the queen when asked. Pixies lived for peace in the world. Maybe it was time to stop running from the past.

"My entire flock was murdered twenty years ago. I only survived because I had awoken from a bad dream and went to the river for a drink. I heard the screams and hid like a coward. When everything was quiet, I flew back to our village, and there was blood everywhere. Everyone I had loved had their wings ripped and their throats slashed. I thought the attackers had left, but a few had stayed back to pillage our wares. If Master Viridian hadn't shown up when he did, I would've died. Maybe I should have. There were so many hearts more pure than mine that deserved to live. I didn't know other flocks had faced the same fate. The news never reached Ethlow."

"Or the master of the house made sure the news never reached you."

My breath was shallow. "It shouldn't have been me who survived. Matron Felca would have been better at all this."

"Guilt over living can weigh you down," Weyland said, but his eyes were far away, as if he understood the guilt of surviving. "But you can't hold yourself back because of it. Without you, we can't break the wards placed around that artifact."

"I... I didn't know it was that bad. Is this artifact that dangerous? What does it do?"

"It is known as the Aethrium Stone, and it can be extremely dangerous in the wrong hands," Weyland admitted. "The fae, pixies, and elves worked together centuries ago to create something that would allow them to stand a chance against the demons that ruled their world. The artifact increases the power of the beholder, so in the hands of a demon king, he could become the emperor of the mortal realms, not just one of five kings and queens."

The implication was hard to miss, but Weyland was wrong. "King Zathrian wouldn't use it to take over. He wants to use it to protect his kingdom."

"Are you sure about that? Your precious king is a demon, and we are known for lying and tricking to get whatever we want. Zathrian outlined his deal with me in incredible detail to make sure I don't betray him, and so the artifact doesn't end up in the hands of one of the other demon rulers."

Weyland made a point that would have convinced most. For centuries, demons had had a reputation for lying, tricking and using others to get their way, but after living at Ethlow, I knew that wasn't true. There were demons like Reamann, who had pure hearts, or like King Zathrian, who fell for a simple human and loved her more than anything. Even the master of the house had his good points.

"I'm sure."

Weyland huffed. "I'm not surprised. If you're not careful, that naivety of yours will get you stabbed in the back."

"I'm not naïve for believing in the good of others. Everyone has good in them, but some haven't had the right light shone on them."

"There is some darkness light will never break, Sunshine."

"I refused to believe that." I held Weyland's gaze, wishing I could be that light for him.

He took a step back, shaking his head. "The world isn't that simple. Get rest tonight. Tomorrow is going to be a busy day. If you have other questions, you can ask them tomorrow." The pirate captain started to walk away, but I couldn't stay silent.

"Can I ask you one more question?" I expected him to brush me off, but he stopped.

Weyland glanced over his shoulder. "What?"

"Did the other night mean anything to you, or were you using me as a way to get off?" It was a stupid question to ask. A demon who loved the seas didn't want to settle down. Sex was different for someone like him than it was for someone like me.

Weyland's face tightened, but I couldn't read the shift in his mood. "Does my answer matter either way?"

Each breath I took was shallow. "Of course, it matters." I didn't know which response was easier to hear. If he told me it was a meaningless night, it would hurt, but it'd be easier to move on. Since there was no future for us, that was the best option, but it didn't stop my heart from yearning for something different.

"Let me ask you something, then. Do you think I was using you?" He stalked back towards me, each step more careful than the last.

"I—" Before I could answer, Weyland grabbed the back of my neck and pressed his mouth against me. The way his lips felt against mine sent my mind racing back to the night he took his time to make me feel incredible.

He pulled back, his silver eye blazing. He braced my head, making it impossible to pull back, not that I wanted to. "If I wanted to fuck someone for pleasure, there are plenty of males and females on this ship that would love for me to take them to bed."

"Males?" I asked, barely able to whisper.

"I don't care what kind of parts someone has. Male, female, both, neither? Doesn't matter to me as long as they are a willing partner. I fuck when I want to fuck, but you... You are more than a one-night stand, Elcy."

"What if I said I was a willing partner?" My heart thundered as the demon spouted words better than what I had imagined.

A low groan escaped the pirate's mouth. "I don't know if I could say no to you, but you should know I can't give you the kind of future you want." Weyland pulled back, making the icy wind brush against my skin. "If you decide that's enough, you know where to find me."

The captain walked away, but my feet refused to follow. I wanted to. I wanted to spend all night with the pirate demon, but he was right. We wanted different futures, and falling into bed with him would only make it more difficult to walk away when this was all over.

Chapter
20

The next day, when I met up with Weyland for training, he acted as if nothing had happened the night before. The invitation was open on his end. If I wanted to spend the night with him, all I had to do was ask, but my head stopped that from happening. I was already in too deep, and I didn't want to make it worse.

So I pretended there was nothing between us as Weyland pushed me to fly. Then I trained with Alre and ended the night with Quinta, looking at the stars. Between everything, the week flew by.

On the seventh day, I woke up to a flurry of activity. I pulled on fresh clothes as quickly as possible to see what was going on. The entire crew rushed to their positions as Weyland shouted orders. My heart thundered, expecting another enemy attack. Instead, I saw an island covered in orange and yellow flowers. The air was colder than it had been for the past several weeks, but the flowers weren't affected by the chill. It was a stunning sight.

"I don't think I've ever seen anything like that," Aukina whispered.

"Dragon's Breath Island," Weyland said. With all the chaos, I hadn't heard him approaching. "It is rumored for its beauty and its danger."

I glanced over my shoulder at the captain. He was in his full gear, including additional weapons strapped to his side.

"What kind of danger?" I asked. After a week of training with Alre, I felt a little more comfortable holding a dagger, but I didn't feel like I could use it properly, especially if I came across a beast or a trained warrior.

"No one knows. The rumors have been enough to stop anyone from coming here, but rumors are always mixed with lies," Weyland said.

"Or anyone who has dared to venture to the island never made it back, losing their stories with their lives," Aukina added. Both Weyland and I glanced at the mermaid in surprise. She shrugged. "It is located in the Calamity Sea. There's a reason the sea got its name, and mermaids talk."

Aukina's explanation only made me feel uneasy.

"If we leave now, we can reach the artifact by midday and be back by sundown. I'm not interested in finding out what lurks at night," Weyland said.

A search party with ten of us took a rowboat to the island. The group consisted of Weyland, the quartermaster, Elmon, Reamann, and five others I barely knew. I bit my tongue when Weyland announced the one-handed elf as one of the search party members. I didn't want to be around him for a second, but I knew it wasn't my place to argue. Aukina and Quinta were both ordered to stay back on the ship, to both of their dismay. The captain didn't want the ship left unattended, and he thought Aukina was best used on the sea.

As we reached the beach, a sweet smell wafted in the air. Between the bright colors and delicious smell, it made it difficult to imagine the island as dangerous. It looked like paradise.

"Don't let your guard down," Weyland grunted. "Just because something looks pretty, it doesn't mean it's harmless." He turned to me and said, "And you stay close. I don't need you wandering off where I need to save you."

My ears turned red, knowing the others in our group heard the order. Did everyone on the crew think I was helpless? I wouldn't have blamed them, but I didn't like the feeling.

"Don't worry. I'll keep a close eye on her," Reamann said, giving me a wink. He had insisted on joining our group when Weyland first gave out the orders, saying he was on the quest as extra protection for me. No one argued against him.

Weyland led the way through the island, taking the natural path between the trees and flowers. The other crew members followed closely behind him. At first, I had tried to stay close to Weyland, but hiking through the unmaintained terrain was harder on my body, especially after a week of training for hours on end. My pace slowed, unable to keep up with the intensity of the captain. I ached to use my wings properly. Flying would have made the difficult terrain a nonissue, but no matter what Weyland and I had tried for the past few weeks, my wings refused to lift me into the air. I had hoped admitting the truth to him would have freed my body from the guilt weighing them down, but it had been the same unsuccessful results.

My breath grew labored with each hour that passed, and a pain stabbed my side. No one else seemed bothered, so I tried to push through without complaint. I didn't want to be the one to slow the group down because I was out of shape.

"Are you okay?" Reamann asked. He stayed by my side the entire time, even as the others pulled ahead.

"Yeah." I didn't say anything else, knowing my strangled breath would give away the truth of my state.

"It's okay to ask for a break," Reamann said. "Aukina struggles with going long distances on land, too. Her body is built for the sea, not the land, just like yours is built for the air."

"I don't want to slow anyone down." I focused on each step, hoping we were getting close to where the artifact was hidden.

"I could carry you instead," Reamann suggested. The offer was sweet, but that sounded mortifying.

"Maybe we can take a quick break," I said. As much as I didn't want to admit my body made me weak, if I kept pushing myself, I'd end up hurt and unable to continue on my own two feet.

"I'll tell the others. Stay here." Reamann ran up ahead to inform the others I needed a break, and I tried not to think about what they'd think of me.

The moment his back was turned, I looked for a spot to rest. There was a fallen log a few feet away with blue moss growing on it. I sat, and my hips popped. Relief flooded my feet, and I focused on my breath, wanting it as calm as possible for when the others came back.

Caw! A crow sat up in the tree next to me.

As I looked at it, I knew it was the same crow from before. The birds all looked the same with their black feathers and beady eyes, but there was something about this bird that felt different.

"I hope you're not here to poop on me again."

"Only if you promise not to insult me." In the blink of an eye, the crow turned into a female.

I screamed and fell back, not expecting a response to my comment.

The stranger chuckled. "That response was better than I was expecting. I thought you'd scream, but falling over is golden." She sat crouched on the branch. Her cropped red hair reflected in the bits of sun that cut through the canopy. Her pale blue eyes practically glowed, revealing the bright colors in the inner ring, one red, one yellow. She was dressed in all black, which made her stand out in the vibrant forest.

I struggled to my feet, not wanting to be in a compromising position in front of the stranger. "You're not a crow."

"Observant little one, aren't you?" Her tone was nothing less than taunting.

I narrowed my eyes. "Excuse me for not expecting a crow to turn into a person."

"Ooh, she's sassy, too." The female plopped onto the tree, letting her feet dangle. She held onto the branch between her legs.

I pressed my lips together, annoyed by the female. "Are you part of Captain Weyland's crew?" It would explain the random crow's appearance at sea, but it was strange no one had talked about someone who could turn into a bird.

"I'm more of a stowaway, but shh, don't tell anyone. It's a secret." She smiled like it was all some big joke.

"If it's a secret, then why did you tell me?"

She shrugged. "Because I wanted to."

"And why wouldn't I tell the captain there is a stowaway on his ship?" I didn't know if she was dangerous, and I didn't want to keep something like that a secret.

"Because I'll kill you if you tell anyone." The amusement lingered in her eyes as she pulled out a dagger.

I swallowed hard and looked around. Reamann should have been back with the others by then. "I should get going." I didn't want to be alone with the stranger.

The moment I tried to step forward, she jumped from the tree, flipping through the air before landing on her feet. She pointed her dagger towards me as she tilted her head.

"You haven't bothered to ask me my name yet. I expected better manners from you. You're always so friendly to everyone."

My body tensed as I stared at the dagger. I didn't know who the female was in front of me, but I got the feeling that she was a little unstable. "What's your name?"

"I'm Kestria. It's nice to officially meet you, Elcy." She held out her hand with the dagger, but then her eyes shifted to the weapon. "Oops. I forgot I was holding that." She flipped the weapon into the sheath strapped to her thigh. She held her hand back out, and when I took it, she shook it wildly.

"It's nice to meet you." I wasn't sure if it was or not, especially with the threats.

"Now that boring introductions are out of the way, let's get straight to business." Kestria circled me like she was ready to strike at any moment.

"What business could you possibly have with me?" I asked.

"That should be obvious, but I'll spell it out for you if I must. You are here to get the Aethrium Stone, and you are the only one who can retrieve it. Once you have it, I need you to give it to me." She stopped and smiled sweetly.

"I'm not going to do that. King Zathrian asked me to help him get it, and I'm not going to betray him or Weyland like that." Kestria was crazy if she thought she could simply ask me to give her the ancient artifact without question.

"Queen Math'ara asked me to retrieve it for her, and Weyland is going to betray you. Might as well betray him first."

My body tensed at her accusation. "Weyland wouldn't betray me. You're making that up."

"Just because he has a nice booty and is good in bed, it doesn't make the demon good-hearted."

I placed my hands on my hips. "Weyland isn't like that."

"Don't be naïve. He's a demon pirate and a male. What more proof do you need?" Kestria shrugged. "But if you don't believe me, take this." She pulled out a gold ring with a blue gem on it. It pulsed with a strange power that was soft and warm.

I hesitated to take the piece of jewelry from her palm. "What's that?"

"A ring of protection. When Captain Booty eventually betrays you, that ring will protect you. When that happens, you'll know that I'm not lying to you."

I took the ring and inspected it. The piece of jewelry felt safe to take, but I wasn't sure if I could trust the female. "I don't know."

"Call me when you do. I'll be close." Before I could answer, Kestria turned into a crow and took off into the sky.

"Elcy!" Weyland called, panic lacing his deep voice.

I slipped the ring into my pocket as the group rushed towards me. I should've dropped it or told the others about it, but as much as I wanted to believe Kestria was lying to me, my gut told me she was telling the truth.

"Where the hell did you go?" Weyland demanded, grabbing my arms. His hands were firm, but it didn't hurt.

I blinked once as confusion set in. "I've been right here. I haven't moved."

"We've been searching for you for ten minutes," Reamann said, his eyes wide with panic.

"I swear I didn't go anywhere," I said, but the stress on everyone's face said otherwise.

Everyone except Reamann and Weyland glared at me as if they didn't believe my story.

Weyland took my hand and pulled me to his side. "You're staying with me from now on. I don't trust this forest."

Chapter
21

The next couple of hours were easier with Weyland's hand in mine. He helped me over fallen branches and guided me to the least encumbered paths. We barely spoke, but his hand in mine made me feel safe. It made me confident that Kestria was making things up to make me doubt the captain. Even if he wanted to betray me, he swore to King Zathrian to protect me.

Despite that, I kept my encounter with the shapeshifter and the ring in my pocket a secret. If I was sure Kestria had been lying, there was no reason to keep the secret from the others, but I couldn't get the words to spill out of my mouth.

"So what are we looking for, exactly?" I asked when my legs started to go numb. I vowed to take more walks once I got back to Ethlow.

"The map I have outlines a cave in the center of the island," Weyland answered. "We should be there soon."

I nodded and returned to focusing on each step. I only had to push through a little longer.

"After all of this, are you really going to go back to the demon king's estate to the same life you had before?" Weyland's question threw me off.

I glanced behind us, but everyone except Reamann had given us space. Reamann pretended like he wasn't listening to the conversation, but I was sure he was—at least I would have been.

"I have a life there. It's not like I have anywhere else to go." Ethlow had been my home for two decades, and knowing pixies had been hunted and killed made me hesitant to want a life away from the demon king's protection.

"You don't seem like the type who would be satisfied living life locked up in an estate, especially with the way your eyes glimmer when you look at the stars."

I didn't know how to respond. The old me had been the one to crave adventure. I loved flying freely through the forest, painting trees, and making my pixie dust decorate the sky. Being on Captain Weyland's ship had reminded me what it was like to feel those things—except the flying. As terrifying as everything had felt, I felt free for the first time in a long time.

"Where would I go if I didn't go back to Ethlow?" I glanced at the captain out of the corner of my eyes, wishing he would ask me to stay with him. Maybe he wasn't the type to settle down, but I could be the type to live freely.

"I hear the kingdom of Valenmae is nice in the winter," Weyland said. "Since the kingdom is by the sea, it stays at the same temperature all year around, and the fae have made the city gorgeous with their architecture skills."

My chest sank at the captain's response. "Queen Math'ara rules Valenmae, doesn't she?"

"She does," Weyland confirmed.

Queen Math'ara was one of the five demon rulers, but I didn't know much about her other than that. If King Zathrian wanted the Aethrium Stone to protect his people, maybe she wanted it for the same reason. It would have put Kestria in the same position I was in.

"You wouldn't want to live a life at sea," Weyland said after a few moments of silence.

His comment surprised me. "Why not?"

"It's hard work, and you never know when you're going to get attacked by another pirate or when the sea will turn on you," he said.

"I thought you controlled the sea."

"Even demons have their limits to their powers."

I hummed loudly. "I didn't realize the dreaded pirate Captain Weyland was so weak. I suppose your horns *are* small for a demon."

Weyland lifted an eyebrow. "I'm a grower, not a shower. You know that, but I can remind you." Something about his tone made butterflies stir in my stomach. The simple comment was enough to question why I had been avoiding his bed.

"Maybe later when there's not so many people around."

"I'd happily take you in front of them if you really don't believe me."

Reamann coughed loudly enough to tell us he was in fact listening, but that didn't lessen the glint in the captain's eyes.

I licked my lips, not wanting to admit how appealing that thought was. I had always thought my needs in the bedroom were plain and simple, but I was questioning if that was true.

Before I could answer the captain, the trees parted, revealing a glade. An opening to a cave sat in the middle of the clearing, but there was no mountain attached to it. It made it look out of place, especially with the black stone that crafted the walls. The stone gave off a strange thrum that made my stomach twist.

"Is that made of tenisium?" Reamann asked. He looked pale as we stood at the edge of the hollow.

"Yes. Another protection set up to stop demons from obtaining the Aethrium Stone," Weyland said.

"What is tenisium?" I had never heard of that material, but Reamann and Weyland were more than aware of it.

"It's a metal that takes away all powers of a demon. Even the most powerful demons become vulnerable if stabbed with the metal," Weyland explained.

"And in a cave made from it?" I asked, a lump forming in my throat. It was clear the captain wasn't prepared for this development.

"Unknown. Tenisium is extremely rare. I didn't know there was this much left in the mortal realm." Weyland was tense, but he didn't look as worried as Reamann.

"We should be careful when we go in there," Reamann said.

"You're not going in with us. I'm not risking more lives than necessary," Weyland said. Reamann opened his mouth to argue, but Weyland lifted his hand to cut him off. "Until we know it's safe, it's stupid to bring the entire crew. If something happens, we need someone to go back to the others for help. Or would you rather your mermaid lover be left waiting, not knowing if you were dead or alive?"

Conflict twisted Reamann's face. He promised to protect me, but the captain made a good point. It wasn't hard to convince Reamann to stay back when Aukina was mentioned. "Fine, but you have to protect Elcy with your life."

"Elcy is the most important one in this group. Without her, this quest would fail. Do you honestly think I would let harm come to her?" Weyland let his magic fill the air, a reminder and a warning. The captain and Reamann were both demons, but Reamann wouldn't stand a chance against Weyland.

Reamann took a step back, but his glare didn't lessen.

"Don't be a fool," Alre said. "Unlike the pixie, you don't have to live."

My eyes widened at the implication. "If you hurt him—"

"You'll what? I know exactly how strong you are after a failed week of training." The quartermaster smirked, knowing I had nothing on him.

"That's enough." Weyland's voice cut through the air, silencing everyone. "We can't waste time if we hope to get back to the ship before dark.

The sun stood proud in the sky, its warmth providing mild relief from the icy temperature. It was a miracle the island wasn't covered in snow.

"Alre, Elmon, follow us. The rest of you, stay here," Weyland ordered.

The captain took my hand and led me towards the cave. As we approached, a nearly invisible shield at the opening of the cave came into view. Streaks of greens and blues reflected off the crystal surface, making it look like a bubble in the sunlight. The air grew thick the closer we got, emitting a strange and ancient magic.

A caw echoed from above as Kestria circled around us. No one but me seemed to notice. I touched the ring in my pocket, its warmth begging me to put it on. If the shapeshifter had been telling the truth, putting on the ring would offer extra protection against the unknowns in the cave. I slipped it on my middle finger. It was a perfect fit, which was a surprise. My fingers weren't the usual size, so jewelry wasn't easy to find.

I should have told the others about the stranger on the island, but there was a small seed of doubt that kept my lips sealed. Kestria had been strange and a little terrifying, but she also seemed like the honest type.

"Alre, Elmon," Weyland said, stopping in front of the cave.

Alre stepped up and placed his hands on the shield. Elmon followed the fae, using the only hand he had left. Everyone looked at me next.

"What's happening?" I asked.

"We need the three types of magic to break down the barrier," Weyland explained.

"I don't know what to do." My wings buzzed as my nerves grew. Magic for pixies was different from others.

"Just place your hand on the shield with some of your pixie dust." Weyland let go of my hand and took a step back.

I folded my wing forward, letting my pixie dust float into my hands. I touched the shield between Alre and Elmon, and power shot through my arms, making my body buzz. The energy that filled me belonged to my ancestors. It was ancient, but I felt the kinship, as if it had been my great, great grandmother who helped create the barrier. Warmth brushed my cheek, telling me it was all going to be okay, and tears slipped from my eyes. I wanted to hold on to that feeling forever.

The shield shattered, falling around us in pieces of magic that looked like glitter. The warmth left my body, making my heart feel empty. For a moment, I had felt the family I had once had, but then it disappeared just as fast.

Alre and Elmon took ragged breaths, as if it had taken everything in them to break the shield. I wiped my eyes, hoping everyone had been too focused on the shield to see my face.

"We did it," Elmon said, a smug smirk filling his face.

"It's not over yet." Weyland's eyes were sharp as he stared into the cave. It was dark, making it nearly impossible to see more than a few feet inside. Ancient power leaked out in full force without the shield containing it, and an uneasy feeling settled in my stomach.

"You two stay here," Weyland ordered, motioning towards the other two.

"They're not coming with us?" Unease filled my bones as I looked at the fae and the elf. As much as I didn't want to be around Elmon, the extra bodies made me feel safer.

"Only you are needed for this next part, Sunshine." Weyland took my hand and squeezed, but it did little to settle my nerves.

It was too late to turn back. We had come this far, and I wasn't about to back down. "Let's do this."

Chapter

22

Weyland's silver eye reflected the light from my pixie dust as he led the way. He walked with confidence, even as the shadows flickered around us. For a while, the ground was flat, but then we reached a set of spiral stairs that clung to the edge of the wall. There was no railing on the right side of the stairs, which meant there was nothing to stop us from falling down the abyss in the center.

My heart raced at the sight, knowing the only way to go was down.

Weyland paused at the top of the stairs, looking back at me. "Will you be okay?" His worry warmed my heart, but it didn't stop the panic from slowly building.

"Do I have a choice?" We both knew the answer to that question. After spending a month on the sea to reach this island, we weren't going to give up and go home because I was afraid of heights.

Weyland squeezed my hand. "I won't let you fall."

I swallowed hard, wishing his words made me feel better. "I will need you to distract me if I'm going to get through this."

Weyland took a step forward, slowly guiding me along. "I can do that, although stairs aren't ideal for what I've been imagining doing to you." The purr in his voice warmed my core.

"I wouldn't sleep with you in a cave, anyway." I rolled my eyes at his flirtation, unsure about how much of it was real and how much was meant to take my mind off the impending doom one wrong step away.

"Is it too dirty for you, Sunshine?"

I kept my eyes on the ground in front of me, not daring to glance at the abyss to my right. "I don't mind it a little dirty." I licked my lips, grateful Weyland couldn't see my face. I didn't want him to know how turned on the conversation was making me, especially when it had barely started.

A low rumble emitted from the captain's chest. "That's good, because I've been dying to know what it feels like to be in your ass."

A strangled noise escaped my mouth, but I wasn't sure if it was from his bluntness or from the idea being more appealing than I thought.

"Have you been thinking about that a lot?" I chewed on my lip as I waited. I had been thinking about what it felt like to have Weyland between my legs ever since it happened the first time.

"I haven't been able to stop thinking about it," Weyland admitted. "I've lost track of the amount of times I thought about walking into your cabin in the middle of the night and taking you until you were screaming my name."

"Why didn't you?" My throat was dry as I thought about the times I had imagined the same thing.

"Because you made your intentions clear, and I don't want to cross that boundary, especially not without your permission."

My heart ached at his admission. The respect he had for me made me wonder why I had believed Kestria's accusations of the captain. Even though Weyland had a reputation for being a vicious pirate, he had shown me repeatedly that he cared about me. If I looked at his actions and filled the gaps with trust, it told me everything I needed to know about the captain.

"Maybe it wouldn't be so bad if we crossed that line again," I said. I was already attached to the pirate. It would hurt when we went our separate ways in the end, but we had a month-long trip back to Ethlow. If my heart was going to break either way, why not spend what time I had with Weyland?

"Don't say things you don't mean." Weyland's voice was strained.

I focused on the stairs in front of me to give myself a moment to sort through my thoughts. "What if I do mean it?" I was walking a dangerous line, but as we climbed down stairs that could lead to our deaths, I wasn't sure I cared.

"If this is you giving me permission, then the moment we are back on that ship, your clothes are coming off, and I don't care who sees me fucking you."

My breath hitched at the thought. The words that danced on the tip of my tongue were dangerous, and I nearly let them slip. We needed to survive this cave before I committed to anything else.

I cleared my throat, knowing I needed to change the subject. I had a hard time thinking about anything other than the throbbing between my legs, and if we continued on the same topic, I'd make bad decisions. "So what's next for you after this quest?"

Weyland took a moment to respond to the change of subject. "Don't know yet. I don't like planning that far ahead. I'll probably go where the sea takes me."

"Do you ever get lonely like that? Never staying in one place for long." I had always wanted to explore the world, but I had loved my flock too much to leave them. Then I was too scared to leave Ethlow. At least at Ethlow, I had friends and beings I cared about.

"Not usually. Sometimes it's nice to have a body to warm my bed, but it's easy to find that."

My chest tightened at the thought. We were adults who had been with others, so there was no reason for it to get to me. "Have you had a lot of bodies in your bed?"

"When you're as old as I am, it's only natural."

"How old are you?" After a certain point, the age of others stopped mattering to me, so I hadn't thought to ask.

"Six hundred, give or take a couple of decades. I stopped keeping track."

"I didn't realize you were so old." It was difficult to determine age with long-lived species. Unlike humans, other beings could be a millennium old and not look a day over twenty-five.

"My age has only made me more skilled." His sultry tone went straight to my core. "And how old are you?"

"Almost a century."

"Then I'm sure you've had quite a few partners." His voice held an edge to it that made the air grow tenser. Was that jealousy or defensiveness?

"Not for a while." I hated admitting that. It made me feel like a prude, but it wasn't like that. I wasn't willing to climb into bed with just anyone, but it was because I didn't trust my heart. I didn't want to fall for the wrong person, but that happened regardless.

"I'm surprised. I would have expected males to be falling over themselves to get your attention with a body like yours."

I blinked, surprise taking over me. "Is that a joke?" My wide hips turned off most of the males at Ethlow. They took one look at my body and decided I wasn't worth their time. Even when I lived with my flock, the same thing happened. I was used to males judging me for my larger body before they spoke a single word to me.

"Why would I joke about that?" Weyland's tone was completely serious. Even if he didn't mind my body, I didn't think he was attracted to it. There was a difference between attraction and tolerance.

"My body isn't the attractive kind."

Weyland stopped walking, making me bump into him. He spun us until my back pressed against the wall. He grabbed my chin, making sure I saw his face, even in the dim light. "Your body is incredible. You don't seem to understand what the thought of it does to me." I felt his hardness press against me, making my breath grow rapid. "If we were anywhere else, I wouldn't hesitate to touch every part of you until you believe just how beautiful your body is."

Weyland shifted, and a rock fell off the edge of the stairs. It was several seconds before the clatter of it hit the ground, reminding me how far of a fall it was. Weyland pulled back slowly, keeping his hand on me. He was well aware of the danger of the stairs, and if the tenisium was affecting him, he couldn't provide the same level of protection as usual.

"Let's hurry, so I can make good on my promise." He pulled me along, keeping the pace steady.

The stairs wound down and down, making it feel as if it'd never end. The air grew warmer with each step, which was a nice relief from the cold. My thighs burned, and I tried not to think about the trip back up those stairs or the trek through the island forest to get back to the ship.

Time blurred as we climbed to the bottom of the chasm. On the center of the floor, there was an altar, and on top of that sat a large opal gem attached to a necklace. The energy shifted, making my body feel lighter as I stared at it. The gem contrasted the dark walls that felt like they were going to swallow us whole.

I stepped towards the altar, my body drawn to it like a magnet, but before I reached it, Weyland's grip slipped from mine. I looked back at him and saw blood running down his ears and nose. He looked strangely pale as he grabbed his stomach and used the wall to keep him upright.

"Weyland," I gasped, rushing to his side. "What happened?" He had been in front of me the entire way down the stairs, and his step had never faltered.

He took several ragged breaths. "It's the tenisium. Demons were never meant to step foot inside here, and it's trying to kill me. A defense against the demon rulers from getting their hands on the Aethrium Stone."

"We have to get you out of here, and fast." If I had known Weyland had been in pain, I would have told him to leave immediately, but he pushed through so that I didn't have to face my fear of heights alone. It was stupid and touching.

"Not without the artifact." Weyland gritted his teeth.

I nodded, forcing myself to turn away from him. The Aethrium Stone sat in the open. It was a little strange. If the elders who built this place went through the effort of building the cave out of a rare metal and put a protection ward on the entrance, it seemed odd for them to leave it out in the open. I stopped in front of the altar and looked around, worried I was missing something. Then my eyes landed on Weyland.

His breath was ragged, and I had never seen him that out of sorts, even after sleeping together. My heart cracked at the sight, and I knew I had to get him out of the cave before the metal killed him like intended.

I reached for the necklace, but there was an invisible barrier around it, similar to the one at the entrance. There was the catch I had been waiting for. I bent my wing forward, letting pixie dust fall directly onto the shield. It melted away as pixie dust poured onto the magic. I reached for the artifact again, just as Weyland shouted, "Wait!" but it was too late. My fingers wrapped around the gold chain, lifting it off the altar.

A crack resounded in my ears, and then I felt the ground shift beneath me. The flooring cracked, and a chunk fell into a true abyss. I dashed forward, but I lost my balance as the cave crumbled. Weyland was next to me in the next second. He grabbed my waist and threw me onto the stairs. The ground collapsed beneath his feet, and I watched as Weyland fell into the darkness.

Chapter
23

I jumped into the darkness without a thought, flying straight towards Weyland. He fell too fast, but I was faster. I wrapped my arms around him, and my wings burst to life. Magic unlike I had ever known pulsed through my veins, and the chasm filled with pixie dust, making it glow brighter than the stars in the sky. My heart pounded as adrenaline pulsed through my veins.

"Elcy," Weyland muttered, his eyes wide as he focused behind me. "You're flying."

I didn't have time to process what that meant as more cracks erupted in the cave, crawling up the walls and making debris fall towards us. If I didn't move, we would both be crushed by the crumbling cave, and the Aethrium Stone would be lost with us. If this was the last hope for Ethlow, I couldn't let it die with us.

I took off, flying as if I had done it every day of my life. I weaved, avoiding chunks of tenisium. My fingers dug into Weyland's back, terrified my arms would give out before we made it to safety. I would not lose Weyland, not before I had a chance to find out if what was between us was real.

We reached the top of the stairwell in a fraction of the time it took to get down, but we barely out raced the destruction behind us. I didn't dare slow, not as I flew over the flat ground. The sounds of stone shattering filled my ears, telling me exactly what was going on without looking back. The entire cave collapsed, and the force of it sent me tumbling forward.

Weyland and I rolled over the ground several times before he ended up on his back with me on top of him. Neither of us spoke, staring wide-eyed at one another as we processed what had just happened.

"Fuck," Weyland muttered, his chest heaving. The color slowly returned to his face now that the tenisium wasn't suppressing his powers. "I thought I was heading straight to the underworld."

"Looks like we're even with saving each other's lives," I said, working to catch my breath.

Weyland smirked. "If I remember correctly, it's three to one, Sunshine. You have some catching up to do."

"Tell you what. I'll give you permission to do whatever you want to me the second we are back on that ship, and we'll call it even." All the hesitations I had before were gone. The moment I thought Weyland was going to die, the walls around my heart shattered. Even if I knew it'd end in heartbreak, I wanted to spend every second of time I had left with him.

"That's a deal I can accept." Weyland reached up and ran his fingers through my hair. He tugged me forward, but before our lips met, shouts from the other crew members filled our ears.

I pushed off Weyland, easily getting to my feet with the use of my wings. My body felt strangely light, a sensation I had missed more than I realized.

"Elcy!" Reamann rushed to my side, looking me up and down. His eyes immediately went to my wings. "You're flying."

"Captain!" Alre helped Weyland to his feet. "What the fuck happened in there?"

Weyland wiped the blood from his nose, but it didn't make him look any better. Between the blood, dirt, and washed out skin, he looked like he had gone to the underworld and back. "When she grabbed the Aethrium Stone, the entire place started to crumble. Another ward was placed to stop someone without the proper abilities from leaving with the ancient artifact." He looked at me and my wings.

"I thought you said I didn't need my wings for this quest," I said, unable to fully process what had nearly happened.

Weyland shrugged. "Guess I was wrong. It happens on the rare occasion." He smirked, his playful nature returning, but there was something else stirring beneath his eyes that was darker.

"But what about the artifact? Did you guys get it?" Reamann asked.

I looked at my fingers curled into a fist. My hand ached from the death-grip on the Aethrium Stone. Even as I carried Weyland to safety, I hadn't let go of the necklace. It was as if my body knew the importance of the artifact in my hand. Slowly, I uncurled my fingers, revealing the opal gem. In the daylight, it looked like a regular piece of jewelry, but the ancient magic filled my veins, making any trace of exhaustion I had felt before disappear.

Alre reached for the necklace, but my hand snapped shut, pulling it close to me. It was an automatic reaction. I didn't want to part with the artifact, and it didn't want to part with me.

The quartermaster's brows lifted in shock. "You don't think you get to hold on to the one thing we have been risking our lives for, do you?"

"This is for King Zathrian, and I plan to hold on to it until I give it to him." My heart thundered as I faced the fae male. Before, I wouldn't have stood a chance against him, but now that I had my wings, I was sure I could out fly the fae.

Reamann stood next to me. His hand hovered over the sword strapped to his side, and tension exploded.

"Maybe I should hold on to it, since my ancestors helped create it," Elmon said.

"Three of us can make that claim. It doesn't make you special," Alre said, puffing his chest.

"Without me, you wouldn't have known where to even find it." Elmon reached for me, but he didn't have a chance to get close.

"Touch her, and I'll take your other hand," Weyland growled, holding a sword between me and the elf.

Elmon instantly tensed, his face souring. He knew exactly what the demon was capable of, and he didn't seem to notice the slight shake in the captain's arm.

"It's a wonder you have a crew willing to follow you when you make threats like that." Elmon spat at Weyland's feet.

Weyland's lips curled at the gesture. "If you feel that way, then you are effectively removed from my crew. Find a different way home."

Elmon paled. "You can't do that. I'll die out here."

"You'll die if you step foot on my ship." Weyland's silver eye darkened to a deep gray as he flared his power. "It's your choice how painful you decide your death will be."

Elmon swallowed hard, stumbling backwards. "You're mad."

"I'm a pirate. It's strange how many seem to forget that. Now run, little elf." Weyland pointed his blade at Elmon.

Elmon shook his head. "Someone is going to take their revenge on you sooner or later."

Weyland laughed. "There's already a line."

The elf turned and took off running in the opposite direction of the ship.

Alre smirked as he and Weyland shared a look. "Shall I?"

"Have fun."

Alre's canines extended as he pulled out a dagger. He held it by the tip and aimed it carefully. He reeled his arm back, and when he released it, the weapon went flying until it embedded itself into Elmon's neck. With a guttural noise, the elf collapsed to the ground.

I gasped, covering my mouth. "You killed him." It was one thing to leave the male to fend for himself on the island, but it was another to kill him.

As if reading my mind, Weyland said, "He was always going to die for touching my treasure. It was just a matter of when. Alre did him a favor by making it quick." He turned to the other crew members, none surprised by the turn of events. "Elcy will hold on to the Aethrium Stone. If anyone tries to take it from her or tries to touch her in any way, your fate will be worse than the elf's. Tell the rest of the crew when we get back."

Weyland held out his hand as an offer to me. I placed the necklace around my neck and tucked it into my shirt. I took his hand, and he squeezed gently, making my heart flutter. No one had ever protected or stood up for me the way Weyland had, and it made me never want to leave his side, even if his violence made me nervous.

Aukina threw her arms around me. "I'm so glad you are okay. And your wings!" She pulled back and admired the glow of the pixie dust pouring off me. It hadn't stopped the entire trek back to the ship.

I spun around, showing off my wings. I couldn't stop my smile from taking over my face. The freedom of flying brought back a lightness I had forgotten I once had.

"She's even faster than me," Reamann said. Aukina ran up to the demon and threw herself at him. They had only been away from each other for part of a day, but they acted as if it had been a week or longer.

Reamann whispered something in Aukina's ear, making her blush. He led her away to the cabins, and it wasn't difficult to discern what they were up to. Without them, other crew members swarmed me, wanting to see my wings.

"Get back to work." Weyland's voice cut through the crowd, but I didn't see him until the crowd thinned. He leaned against the railing, his gaze locked on me. My body flushed, remembering the things he said he'd do to me before we nearly died.

Weyland pushed off the railing and stalked towards me. My heart raced, wondering if he'd make good on his words from before. When he reached me, a smirk graced his lips.

"You have two choices," he said. "I can take you right here, so the entire crew knows you're mine, or I can take you to my bed and do things no other male has ever done to you before." His eyes smoldered at the choices presented to me.

I licked my lips, confused by how turned on both options made me. "Take me to your bed."

Weyland's silver eye glimmered. He leaned in, stroking my cheek. "Good choice, because I might have killed anyone who dared to look at your bare skin."

Chapter 24

Weyland led me to his room, both of us silent in anticipation. He locked every door leading to his private quarters to ensure no one would bother us. If they did, they might lose a few fingers, if not more. The moment we were alone, Weyland let go of my hand and turned towards me.

"Sit on the bed," he ordered.

My body obeyed without objection. I tucked my knees under me and placed my hands on my thighs as I waited for the next command. Weyland pulled off his jacket before folding it over the chair in the corner. His shirt came off next, revealing his rippling muscles and the dark chain tattoos covering his skin. He left his black leather pants on as he approached the bed.

"Your turn, Sunshine." His cocky grin drove me wild.

I didn't need more of an explanation to understand what he meant. I pulled my shirt and brassiere off, carefully navigating the cloth around my wings. My breasts fell free, and his eyes immediately went to them.

"All of your clothes," he said, his eyes flicking back to mine.

I reached for the necklace holding the Aethrium Stone, but Weyland stopped me.

"Not that. Everything but the artifact. I want you to keep that on you at all times. Understood?"

I nodded, sliding my hands down to work on removing my bottoms next. My heart thundered as I sat completely nude in front of the demon. Even though he had reassured me that he liked my body in the cave, it was difficult to push past a lifelong insecurity.

Weyland stroked his chin as he looked me over. "Good girl. I want you to follow all of my instructions just like that. Understood?"

I nodded quickly. His sultry voice made me want to do anything he asked.

He grabbed my chin and leaned in close. "I need you to listen to this next part closely. If I do anything you don't like, or if it goes too far, say 'goblin.'"

"Goblin?" I giggled. It was strange to think about that word in this context.

"This isn't a joke, Sunshine. The things I have planned for you go beyond the regular vanilla sex you are likely used to. If you say 'goblin,' I will instantly stop what I'm doing. Understood?"

I swallowed, my giggles disappearing. I nodded, eager to learn what Weyland had planned for me. He wasn't wrong about the sex in my previous relationships being vanilla.

Weyland kissed my lips lightly. "Good girl." He tilted my head and kissed down my neck, making my body shiver. His fingers traced my collarbones until they reached my breasts. He squeezed them gently, and I hummed from the pleasure. He took his time, making my body heated and my core slick with anticipation.

His fingers dipped between my legs. He stroked my clit before circling back to my entrance. He teased the hole, but he didn't push inside like I desperately craved.

"Are you on any contraceptives?"

My heart thundered. There was a healer on the ship, but I hadn't bothered asking about that since I hadn't planned on having sex with the captain or anyone else. I should've known better after last time. I shook my head, afraid all of this would stop.

"Looks like I'll get your ass after all." He nipped my lip before he pulled back, removing both his hands from my body. A whimper escaped my lips, which only made the demon smirk.

"Patience, Sunshine."

Weyland lifted his arms, and the chain tattoos that ran from his pecs to his arms rose from his skin, coming alive. Thick, black chains floated in front of the demon pirate, only attached to his body at the spot between his shoulder blades, and his silver eye glowed as his power poured from him.

"Hold your hands above your head," he ordered. I lifted my hands, which made me aware of how it made my heavy breasts pull up. They had never been perky, the extra weight pulling them towards the ground, but Weyland didn't care.

With a flick of his wrist, the chains darted for my hands. I flinched from the sudden movement, but it didn't prevent the living tattoos from wrapping around my wrists, tying them together. It was a snug fit, but it didn't hurt.

"I think I like you tied up." The demon looked at my wrists before shifting his gaze lower. "I think you need more."

Weyland grabbed my hands and spun me around on the bed as if I weighed nothing. The chains around my wrists pulled forward and tied around the headboard, forcing me on my elbows and knees. More chains wrapped around my ankles, forcing my legs to spread. My heart raced with excitement at the position. I was at the demon's mercy, and I loved it.

He ran his hand over my ass, shifting between kneading it and gently stroking the cheek. "You have no idea how many times I've thought about your ass." *Smack!*

I yelped at the sudden motion, but it was only a slight sting. Weyland leaned forward and kissed the spot. Pleasure replaced any essence of pain, and my core throbbed with desire. Weyland repeated the same motion two more times, smacking my ass before kissing the pain away. It made my head fuzzy from the new sensations.

Weyland shifted behind me, but in that position, I couldn't see what he was doing. He grabbed both of my ass cheeks before pulling them apart. It was the most exposed I had ever been, but he didn't leave me like that for long. He dipped his tongue into the apex of my thighs, starting with my clit until he moved up through my pussy until he reached my ass. My body jolted as he swirled around my puckered hole. I had barely had a tongue in my pussy, let alone my ass, but the more he stroked the area, the more I enjoyed it.

Weyland replaced his tongue with a finger and pushed in gently. The moan that came out of my mouth surprised me. He worked the hole, slowly adding additional fingers, making sure I was open and prepared for him. When he reached around and teased my clit while using his fingers to pump in and out of me, I lost it. My whole body clenched, unexpected pressure building.

"That's it, Sunshine. Come for me." His words were a command my body was desperate to follow. An orgasm rippled through me, making my muscles clench and unclench more powerfully than when Weyland had been in my other entrance.

Before I had fully recovered, I heard Weyland pulling down his pants, letting them drop to the floor. He pulled my hips back and then lined himself up with my ass. Pushing in slightly, he let me adjust to his size. He was bigger than his fingers had been, so I was grateful for the slow pace.

He pushed in deeper, a groan rumbling from his chest. "Your ass feels better than I imagined." With a quick motion, he pushed all the way into me until his body was flushed with mine. It was a different sensation than when he was in my pussy, but in the best way possible. I had never thought anal could feel better than regular sex, but the demon proved me wrong.

It wasn't long before Weyland began thrusting in and out of me. His fingers dug into my hips as he slammed into me hard and fast, nothing like the gentleness he used last time. He kept up his pace, going as deep as he could each time. When he got close, he reached around to my front and rubbed my clit. I was at his mercy, unable to move with the chains keeping me still.

My toes curled as Weyland coaxed another orgasm from me. As I pulsed around him, he slammed into me one last time, spilling his seed in my ass. He leaned forward, kissing my shoulders as he caught his breath.

The chains unwrapped from my wrists and ankles, and Weyland pulled me into him. He kissed my forehead and stroked my hair. "Are you okay, Sunshine?" His voice was surprisingly sweet after what had just happened.

"I'm wonderful."

He kissed me again. "Good."

I traced the tattoos that had returned to his chest. "So that's why you chose chains."

Weyland chuckled. "I don't like to break them out the first time with someone. Some run at the sight, but I knew you could handle it. I'm just surprised you enjoyed that so much. You're kinkier than I expected."

My cheeks turned red with embarrassment. "Am not."

"You came harder with me in your ass than your pussy, Sunshine. You can't lie about this." Before I could argue, he pulled me into a deep kiss, and I gave up the need to fight him. "Let's get you cleaned up."

"Or we could go again." I bit my lip and looked away.

Weyland hardened beneath me. "Such a dirty girl." He nipped my ear, and I knew it was going to be a long night.

My body startled awake, but the arm draped over my waist reminded me of where I was and what had just happened repeatedly. My body was tired, but it felt lighter than it had in a long time.

Weyland breathed deeply in his sleep. The steady rise and fall of his chest was comforting, and I knew then I couldn't leave him. There was no doubting it. I wanted to stay by Weyland's side as he ventured across the seas. I wanted to experience those adventures and see the world, but most of all, I wanted to wake up with him by my side. It wasn't the life I had imagined for me recently, but it was the life I had imagined when I was a child. I was tired of holding myself back because I was the one who survived.

It was time for me to live my life and pursue real happiness.

I kept my laugh to myself. I never expected exuberance to come from a pirate or a demon, let alone both.

I was too awake to fall back asleep, so I untangled myself from the demon's arms, careful not to wake him. After the day and night we had, he needed his rest. Even if he pretended otherwise, I knew the tenisium cave had taken nearly everything from him. How he managed to get back to the ship and do all of that to me was a mystery.

I pulled on a heavy coat before stepping out onto the ship deck. The chilled air caused my breath to cloud my face, but I only planned on being outside for a few moments. The moon lit my way as I climbed onto the quarterdeck. I expected Quinta to be at the helm, but she was nowhere in sight. All the crew must've been resting after the celebration that occurred after our successful mission.

I looked up at the stars and smiled as they decorated the sky. Staying with Weyland meant getting to see the stars nightly, as long as the weather permitted. Ethlow didn't offer the same freedom. I'd go back to the demon king's estate, give him the ancient artifact, and then pack up my stuff before committing to a life at sea with the dreaded demon pirate Captain Weyland. I hadn't spoken to him about my plan yet, but I was sure he wouldn't argue—not after everything we did.

I scanned the stars, looking for Mystic Sigil and Phoenix Rising to find my way home. The stars glittered in the sky, but something was off. I combed through my memories of my lessons with Quinta, hoping I was wrong, but everything I remembered made it clear I wasn't. The ship was going the wrong way. It wasn't going back to Ethlow.

It had to be a mistake. I searched the deck, hoping to find someone to tell them they had to correct the ship before we wasted an entire night going the wrong direction, but the deck was eerily empty. Weyland could fix it, or he'd be able to find Quinta to do it for him.

I burst through the door to the captain's office, but I froze when I saw a figure sitting at his desk. I had only seen her once, but it was impossible to forget the face of the pirate captain who had attempted to kidnap me.

"Irelina," I gasped. I took a breath to scream for Weyland, but a hand covered my mouth as a figure emerged from the shadows.

"Don't bother screaming," the mermaid said, inspecting her nails closely. "Even if someone heard you, it'd do no good. I am an invited guest on this ship, after all."

Chapter
25

M y body tensed. Captain Irelina was lying. It was the only explanation. Weyland would have never invited her on the ship after what she tried to do. He hated her. If I got his attention, he'd stop the mermaid and keep me safe. He was only a room away. A loud noise would be enough. I couldn't scream with the hand over my mouth, but if I waited for the right moment, I could kick something over.

"I see those thoughts churning in your head, but they are of no use." Irelina placed her feet on the desk and leaned back. "Your precious Weyland is the one who betrayed you. Don't believe me? I'll prove it." She lifted her hands to her mouth and shouted, "Oh, Weyland!"

I couldn't breathe as I watched the door to his room. There were shuffling noises from the other side. I waited for him to burst through the door and put Irelina's lies to the grave. He wouldn't betray me, not after everything he had done for me. The door swung open, and Weyland froze in the threshold between rooms. He had only bothered to put his pants on, leaving his torso exposed. He scanned the situation, keeping his face neutral. After a moment, he leaned against the doorframe, relaxing. It was the opposite of what I had expected.

"Irelina, what the fuck do you want?" Irritation flooded his eyes.

I held my breath, refusing to lose hope. He was buying time to rescue me.

"I was hoping you could tell little Sunshine here what we discussed on my ship before you blew it up." Irelina's smile was vicious, made worse by the sharp teeth filling her mouth.

Weyland's eyes flicked to mine, and for a moment I swore I saw regret, but then his face returned to a neutral expression, making me question what I saw.

"I don't have time for this," he growled. He didn't look at me again.

"Don't you want the pixie to know that you made an agreement with me? As soon as you used her to get your precious treasure, then you'd turn her over to me in exchange for free exploration of the Calamity Sea without interruption from the Silverstar Mermaids. Is this a lie?" Irelina looked at me as she waited for Weyland's response. It was as if she wanted to see the moment my trust fell apart.

"No," Weyland grunted. "Now get your feet off my fucking desk."

Irelina ignored his order. "I see you finally fucked her. Decided to get your dick wet before it was too late after all. My only surprise is you didn't do so sooner."

My chest was on the verge of collapsing. Weyland traded my life for immunity. Everything he did and said to me was a lie. All those times he saved my life... Every time he called me his treasure... No. That was right. To him, I was an object to be traded, just like a gem or ancient artifact.

"Don't cry, pixie." Irelina stood and walked over to me. She placed her hand on my chin. "I'm sure I can find someone more skilled and bigger to fuck you. You might be my slave, but I'll treat you well if you do as I say."

A snarl erupted from Weyland's chest. It was almost enough to make me believe he cared about me, but if that was true, he would have stopped this. He wouldn't have made the deal in the first place. I watched him, waiting for him to look at me, to say it was all a lie, but his eyes never met mine, as if he didn't care what I thought.

"Get out, before I kill you." Weyland's voice was low and deadly.

Irelina lifted her hands, wiggling her fingers. "It was a pleasure doing business with you. I look forward to our partnership."

The metal cage Irelina had her crew put me in was barely big enough to fit my wings. It was tucked away in a random cabin on her ship, away from any eyes. I was grateful for the privacy as I sobbed through my broken heart. I was nothing less than a fool. From the beginning, I knew my heart would break if I got into bed with Weyland, but I hadn't expected it to hurt like this. For a moment, I had let myself believe there was a real future with the captain, but he was a demon and a pirate. Separately, he had a chance, but together...

I had believed in him, trusting his actions. Everyone had good in them—or so I thought.

I sobbed until there were no tears left. Hours passed by in a numb blur, and I drifted to sleep when I had no energy left. Soft clicking noises stirred me awake. I lifted my pounding head and jumped when I saw a rat staring at me. I would've screamed if my throat hadn't been so raw.

"I suppose you couldn't break me out of here, huh?" My voice cracked. My throat was parched after hours of crying and no access to water.

The rat tilted its head. It almost looked cute, especially with its one red eye and one yellow one. I hadn't seen a rat with heterochromia before. There was something strangely familiar about it.

In the blink of an eye, the rat shifted to a female. Kestria sat cross-legged in front of me, holding her knees. "I could get you out if I felt like it."

I jumped and screamed, slamming my back into the metal bars. "Kestria."

She cackled, rocking back and forth. "You are too easy to scare. I think I like you."

I pressed my hand on my chest, my heart thundering. "Because I'm easy to scare?"

"You're gullible, too."

I glared at the shapeshifter. "Gee, thanks."

"You're welcome!" Either she didn't catch my sarcasm, or she ignored it.

I wanted to be mad at her, but the anger didn't come. I had spent all of my emotions on the demon pirate, and I felt too drained to care about the shapeshifter's teasing. "Why are you here?"

Kestria's laughter faded as she stilled her body. "I told you he'd betray you."

My gut twisted, hating that she was right. There was a small voice that had wondered if it was true, but it was easier to believe the male who repeatedly acted like he cared. "I should've believed you."

"Yes, you should have. I told you, I don't lie."

"But how did you know?" I refused to believe that Weyland's demonic nature had been enough to convince her. She had been too sure of herself.

"I overheard him making a deal with Irelina during her attack. It's the advantage of disguising yourself as an animal. People assume they aren't listening, which makes my line of work easier."

Kestria's explanation only confirmed Irelina hadn't been lying, either. There was only one male who had been lying, which made my heart wrench.

"What line of work?" It was easier to ask the shapeshifter questions than to think about Weyland's betrayal.

"I'm an assassin and spymaster. Thief when asked." She answered without hesitation.

"For someone in that line of work, you're dangerously honest." Knowing Kestria's profession should've made me nervous, but I didn't have the energy to care.

Kestria shrugged. "Whether my targets know I'm coming or not doesn't hinder my results. I have yet to find someone to match my prowess." She hopped to her feet and grabbed the metal bars separating us. "Do you want freedom?"

I narrowed my eyes slowly. "What kind of question is that? No one would want to stay in a cage this small, knowing they are a prisoner."

"I can free you for a price." Kestria smiled, innocence filling her face. Despite being an assassin, a thief, and a spymaster, there was something about the shapeshifter that made me trust her—not that I trusted my instincts after Weyland's betrayal.

"What kind of price?" As tempting as it was to agree instantly, the one thing I learned from being on a pirate ship was that everything came at a cost.

"Give me the Aethrium Stone, and I'll make sure you escape this ship." Kestria's eyes moved to the area between my breasts.

My hand immediately went to the opal pendant. I had forgotten the artifact hung around my neck. Weyland was the one who ensured I kept it on me. It made no sense that he would do that knowing Irelina was coming for me, but maybe he hadn't expected the female pirate to come in the middle of the night.

As much as I wanted freedom, the shapeshifter asked for the one thing I couldn't give. "I can't, not when I promised King Zathrian I would bring it back to him." I hoped that someone would come for me once they learned of Weyland's betrayal. Aukina was a mermaid, which meant she could navigate the sea and find me. Or she could go to King Zathrian and tell him what happened. Someone would come for me. It was just a matter of when that'd happen.

"Boo." Kestria pushed out her lower lip. "I thought you'd be more willing to work with me after getting betrayed."

"Why don't you just take it from me instead of trying to bargain for it?" I asked.

Kestria's eyes lightened. "That's not a bad idea."

My heart stopped beating. I should've kept my big mouth shut.

Kestria let out a sharp laugh. "I knew you were gullible." She waved a finger at me, beckoning me to move closer. I hesitated, but then she added, "Please?"

I pushed myself to my feet, unsure if I was making a mistake. I leaned in until the tiny details in Kestria's eyes were clear. "Yes?"

"I'm not going to take the artifact from you just yet, because you need it more right now, but you should know I will be back for it. I've been hired to do a job, and I refuse to be anything less than perfect." She squeezed my hand, reminding me of the ring on my finger. "Get home safe, Elcy, and I'll see you there."

Before I could respond, she shrank into her rat form and scurried off just as the door opened. I didn't know what to make of the assassin, but I knew that wasn't the last time I was going to see her.

Two large males strode into the room and came straight for me. Either they didn't notice the rat running behind the supply crate, or they didn't think anything of a harmless rat.

"The captain wants to see you."

Chapter 26

S hackles were placed around my hands and a chain was attached to them, making it easy for the male crew members to lead me to the top of the deck. I walked, unsure if they knew my wings worked or not. If they didn't know, I might have been able to use it to my advantage.

Irelina sat on the railing of the ship, letting her feet dangle over the side. "Bring her to me." The captain held out her hand without looking back. The male placed the chain in the mermaid's hand, and Irelina yanked the metal, making me stumble forward until my body hit the railing.

For a moment, I wondered what would happen if I shoved the captain over the ship. My wings weren't encumbered, which would have allowed me to fly to freedom. The problem was the expansive sea before us. Without a place to go, my wings would tire, and I'd end up stranded in the middle of the ocean.

"I'm sure you're wondering why I would bargain with the male I hate for a pixie."

"It doesn't matter why," I said. It wasn't hard to guess Irelina's motives. "Money, power? It's the same motive for all pirates, isn't it? Capture the only known pixie in the mortal realm and use her for your own benefits." Anger tightened my throat as I thought about Weyland's betrayal. Every moment between us was tainted, making it impossible to tell what was real and what wasn't.

"Don't cry over that bastard. Trust me, he's not worth it." There was something about Irelina's tone that made my body freeze.

"Have the two of you..." I couldn't bring myself to finish that question. Even after Weyland's betrayal, I didn't like thinking about him with others.

"We've done some very dirty things together, yes. You'd be surprised about how many males go crazy for a woman with a tail and how many of them want to fuck a half fish in that form. But you know how it is. A pirate never settles." Irelina flipped her hair, and I felt like crying all over again. The mermaid was beyond gorgeous. She was the type anyone would fall for from sight alone.

I felt sick. "What do you want?" I wanted to crawl back in the cage and cry where no one could see me.

"I want to make a deal with you. If you promise to supply pixie dust willingly, I will make sure you live a good life, at least as good of a life a prisoner could have. You'll have your own room with sheets made of the finest silk. I'll provide you with decadent meals made by the realm's best chefs. You'll have your pick of males to sleep with, women too if you swing that way." Irelina's offer was appealing, but there had to be a catch.

"And what's the alternative?"

The mermaid yanked my chains, making my wrists scream in pain. "You don't want to know the alternative." Her voice was lethal, sending a shiver down my spine.

"It sounds like there's not much of a choice." My body deflated. Less than a day ago, I was dreaming of a future filled with freedom. Now, I was faced with the choice of cooperating as a slave, or something much, much darker.

"Everyone has a choice. If you agree to make a deal with me, I will place my signet on your skin, and you'll be mine forever. That's the advantage of having demon blood running through my veins. If you agree to this deal, you won't be able to betray me." She offered me her hand. Her nails were painted red and shaped into points as sharp as her teeth.

A life of luxury in exchange for giving up my freedom, or a promise of pain and torture until someone came to get me—if someone came for me. I couldn't handle the thought of being tortured. I wasn't strong like that, but the thought of giving up my freedom felt worse.

I shook my head, fighting back tears. I thought I had cried enough for a lifetime, but my emotions rose to the surface in unbearable waves. "I don't know."

Irelina curled her fingers, her knuckles popping from the motion. Her face dropped, ire flashing across it. "This is the only time you'll receive this offer. Accept it now, or expect to be miserable for the rest of your long life."

The pressure made me feel like I should take her deal. If I was wrong and no one came for me, I didn't know if I could survive more than a few weeks, depending on what Irelina had planned. The only thing stopping me was knowing what it tasted like to be free. I finally had use of my wings, and if I took her deal, I would never know what it felt like to fly through the forest, the wind whipping through my hair.

"Tick-tock. Tick-tock, Sunshine."

"Don't call me that," I snapped.

Irelina pulled my chains towards her and hooked a finger around a tendril of my hair. "What? Can only people who fuck you call you that? I wouldn't be opposed. You are quite beautiful."

If Irelina had flirted any other time, I would've been flattered, but it felt like an insult. "I don't sleep with bitches who think they can pressure someone into slavery."

Irelina slapped her hand across my face, her nails slashing my skin in four straight lines. "How dare you?" She grabbed me by the throat, digging her nails into my neck.

As my lungs struggled to obtain oxygen, panic washed over me. This was only the beginning of what would come of me if I didn't agree to Irelina's proposition. I clawed at her hand, desperate to get free from her grasp, but she wasn't budging.

"You made the biggest mistake of your life, pixie. I'm going to make sure you suffer every—"

A blue light flashed, emitting from the ring Kestria gave me. A blast of warm air pushed Irelina off me, allowing me to stumble free and catch my breath. The captain lost her balance and fell into the water below. I scrambled to the edge, peering down at the hat floating in the water. There were no signs of the captain's red hair.

Boom.

A scream escaped my lips as I covered my ears from the unexpected explosion. My body shook, fear ripping through me. Another cannon exploded as a familiar ship approached. The black sails with a white stripe flew towards us, and the captain with matching hair stood at the helm of the ship. My heart thundered at the sight of him and the others. Out of everyone to come for me, they were the last ones I expected. Aukina hopped onto the railing of the ship and dove into the water. Three more cannons rang out, two of the explosions hitting Irelina's ship and making it rock.

I clung to the railing, barely able to stay on my feet. Chaos erupted as Irelina's ship lurched into action. The crew barely noticed me with an enemy ship at their heels. I had to leave now before that change. My wings roared to life, and I lifted into the air, but someone grabbed my ankle, slamming me back to the ground. I kicked my other foot, attempting to free myself, but it felt like kicking metal. The body of the male fae was sturdy, and he dug his fingers into my ankle as if his life depended on it. It likely did.

A screech echoed from above. A dark figure flew through the air like a torrent, aiming straight for the male. Quinta landed on top of the male, plunging a dagger through his chest. She grabbed his head until it twisted with a loud crack! She looked at me with a wild gleam.

"It's good to see you, pixie."

"You have no idea how true that is." My throat swelled as relief washed through me.

Battle cries from Irelina's crew echoed around us, the harpy's entrance drawing attention to us.

"Can you fly?" Quinta asked. I nodded. "Then I suggest you do so now." She pulled out two daggers and faced the group of ten coming for us.

"You're outnumbered." I wasn't any good at fighting, so I knew I'd only cause her issues, but I didn't want to leave her alone when she was here to rescue me.

"Just the way I like it. Now go before they decide to bring out archers." Quinta screeched and ran into the fray.

I took off before I saw the results of the battle. Quinta was strong and could handle herself, unlike me. I flew as fast as I could towards the ship I had become familiar with for the past month. It was strange flying with my hands bound, but I wasn't about to waste the opportunity.

Reamann's orange hair grew clear as I neared the ship. He held a bow with an arrow locked into place. "Get down!" he shouted.

I didn't wait to find out why he gave the order. I changed my angle for the deck, but I didn't have time to slow. I crashed into a body, and muscular arms caught me, stopping me from face planting. The familiar scent of the sea water and cedarwood filled my nose. Relief flooded my system, but it was quickly replaced by anger as I faced the black and silver-eyed pirate.

"You can call me every name in the book later, Sunshine. Once we are safe, I promise to explain everything. Right now, I need you to trust me and hide in my office." Weyland helped me to my feet, his hands lingering on my arms.

I wanted to yell at him, but as more cannon fire erupted around us, I decided to trust him, even if it was one last time. I nodded, agreeing to his terms.

"One last thing." He leaned in, and for a moment, I thought he was going to kiss me. Instead, he grabbed the chains and snapped them with his bare hands, as if they were made of tree branches. "Go."

"I thought we had a deal, Weyland." Irelina's voice made me freeze. She pulled herself onto the railing of the ship, easily flipping her tail over the edge. Wind blasted against her, replacing her fin for legs. She stood naked on the deck, but she didn't care.

Reamann aimed his bow at the mermaid, but Irelina waved her hand, sending the weapon and the guardsman flying.

Weyland stepped in front of me, his body growing as he shifted into his demon form. "And I completed my end of the bargain."

Irelina snarled. "If you don't give me the pixie back now, I will slit the throat of every crew member beneath you. Then I'll make you watch as I torture the pixie."

Weyland's roar made the deck shake. "You forget one thing. I'm stronger than you." His tattoos came to life, and the chains floated in the air, ready to strike. "Go now, Sunshine. I don't want you to see this."

"Yes, it'd be a shame for her to watch me destroy you," Irelina said.

Weyland snapped a chain towards the other captain, but with the help of the wind, Irelina easily dodged.

"Now, Elcy!"

My feet took off, afraid to spend another second near Irelina. The thought of being locked in a cage on her ship turned my blood to ice. As soon as I reached Weyland's office, I locked the door behind me. Hiding felt familiar, but I didn't dare step onto the deck knowing what Irelina had planned for me. Time stretched as explosions and cries rang out, and it felt as if the fighting would go on forever. When silence filled the air, I wanted to cry. I didn't know how many had died in the fight to protect me, and I didn't know if I was safe—not after Weyland let Irelina take me.

But he came to rescue me.

Confusion filled my head, and I didn't know what to think of the captain or the situation.

When the silence stretched on outside the safety of Weyland's office, my heart pounded, terrified to find out who won and who died. I waited for someone to tell me it was safe to come out, but as the minutes ticked by, I couldn't wait any longer. I opened the captain's door, afraid I'd see the worst. The ship was damaged, and there were bodies on the ground, but most of the bodies were ones I didn't recognize. I looked for Irelina's ship, but it was nowhere in sight, along with its captain.

Loud footsteps echoed throughout the deck, and every living crew member turned their gaze towards the pirate captain. Blood soaked his ripped shirt, and his hat was missing, but he was alive.

It took everything in me not to run towards him. I wanted to be in his arms more than anything, but I couldn't let myself go there again. It was too risky. Not when he let Irelina take me.

Weyland continued towards me, stopping only when he was directly in front of me. Dark circles hung beneath his eyes. His body was strained, as if he was holding himself back. He lifted his hand, brushing under my jawline. "You're hurt."

The blood from the scratches Irelina gave me had dried, but the sting lingered. My focus shifted to Weyland's chest. The gash on his chest looked like it was from a bladed weapon with how clean the marks were.

"So are you."

"Elcy! Thank Artagatis you're okay." Aukina was back in her human form, and Reamann was by her side. He had a few cuts on him and a black eye, but nothing he wouldn't live through.

"You came for me," I whispered, tears bubbling in my eyes.

"There was never a moment I wasn't going to come after you," Weyland said.

My heart thundered, wanting to believe him, but there was too much I didn't understand.

Aukina took my hand. "We should clean your wounds before they get infected."

"I'll do it." Weyland used the voice of a commander, but it didn't phase Aukina or Reamann.

"I think it's best that she stays with us." A protective growl emitted from Reamann's mouth. His eyes burned with hatred as he glared at the captain. There was a lot that happened while I was gone between them, but I could ask about that later. There were more pressing questions at the forefront of my mind.

I placed a hand on Reamann's arm. "It's okay. I need to talk to him."

Reamann's jaw feathered, but he kept his mouth shut. Aukina looked uncomfortable, but she didn't argue. "We'll be close by if you need anything."

I nodded, grateful for my two friends. "I'll be okay, but thank you."

"I have supplies in my room," Weyland said. He gestured towards his office, careful not to touch me.

"No. I want to go to my room." I didn't trust myself in Weyland's bedroom, not with the memories that lingered there.

I took the lead, holding my head high and hoping I wouldn't crumble in front of the captain.

Chapter 27

I sat on my bed as Weyland knelt on the ground, cleaning the scratches on my cheek. Neither of us spoke as he focused on dressing the wounds. I wanted to ask him a hundred different questions, but I held back, wishing he would be the first to speak.

When he was done, our eyes met, and I couldn't breathe. Pain filled his eyes, but he was the one who betrayed me.

"Do you want to call me names first, or do you want my explanation?" Weyland asked. He didn't move from his knees. His fingers brushed against the bruises on my wrists, his face tightening at the sight.

His question was harder to answer than I had anticipated. The logical part of me said to give him a chance to explain, because it might make the feeling of betrayal go away, but there was a knot in my chest filled with anger.

"How about I call you names, and then you can explain? If I don't like what you say, I'll call you more names."

"Do your worst."

I stood, moving away from the demon. I wasn't sure I'd be able to say everything on my chest while looking at him.

"You are the most selfish male I have ever met, and I know you are a pirate and demon, but I don't give a shit. You pretended to like me to get me to trust you, and that's just fucked up, because I would have trusted you without spreading my legs, because I believe there is good in everyone. You took advantage of my kindness, and you took advantage of my vulnerabilities, and for what?" I wrapped my arms around myself and took a slow breath.

Weyland's eyes burned as he stared at me, but he kept his mouth shut, waiting for me to finish.

"You're worse than males like Elmon. At least he was clear with his nefarious intentions, but you're a liar. You took it too far, because my attention made you feel good. You have spent your life at the sea, not because it calls to you, but because you don't have to care about anything or anyone but yourself. For a moment, you felt what it could be like to share a life with someone—with me—and you threw it away. Not because you're power hungry, but because you were too scared to feel something real. I could call you an asshole, but that wouldn't mean anything. What you are is a craven charlatan, and you deserve to be alone for the rest of your insipid life."

It was a miracle I wasn't crying. Even in anger, tears often flowed, but I was beyond upset.

Weyland's chest rose and fell in ragged breaths. His eyes grew heavy as he waited to see if I'd talk more. "Is it my turn?"

I shrugged, trying to hide my shaking hands. "Do your best." I wanted Weyland to explain away the pain in my chest, because I wasn't sure I'd be able to handle the journey back to Ethlow with the feelings weighing me down.

"You're right. I am a craven charlatan—even though those words are fancier than I would have used. I am a pathetic scoundrel for using you the way I did, and I probably deserve a lonely, insipid life—as you would say."

My heart wrenched. Weyland agreeing with me meant he was in the wrong. I had hoped he had some sort of grand explanation that would magically make everything okay, but that wasn't the case.

"I never should have made that deal with Irelina, but when I realized how much she wanted you, I couldn't help myself from seizing an opportunity."

I scoffed, rolling my eyes.

Weyland closed the distance between us and grabbed my arms. "It's not what you're thinking, Elcy. I always intended to come after you. I wanted to use you as bait to learn where Irelina's home base is. Then I could take her out for good, because she is a slippery eel who continues to escape me. But when I made that deal, I never expected to care for you. I never thought I'd start falling in love with you. If I had known that, I never would have considered a deal with that wretched fish."

I couldn't breathe. I hadn't expected Weyland to admit to those kinds of feelings, but it was hard to accept them as true. "And you expect me to believe that you have feelings for me? How am I supposed to know if everything you're saying is just another lie? If you realized you made a mistake making that deal, why didn't you stop her from taking me? Better yet, why didn't you tell me about it before it happened?"

"Because I'm a craven charlatan. You are right. About all of it. As much as I love the sea, I also feel safe here. I never stick with the same person for more than a few weeks because I'm afraid that if they see what's truly in my heart, they'll realize I'm a monster on the inside. It's easier to be alone, but it is impossible to stay away from you. You are a light that shines against my darkness, and I want to follow you anywhere. I know I should have told you about the deal with Irelina sooner. I thought about it when I told you to keep the ancient artifact with you, but I was afraid you'd reject me once you learned the truth. I thought I had more time, but Irelina came sooner than I expected. I'm sorry."

"Did you at least get what you wanted from Irelina?" I couldn't look him in the eyes. I wanted to accept his apology more than anything, but I couldn't.

"No, because that would have involved weeks with you in her hands, and I couldn't handle a single day without you."

"You're an asshole."

"I know."

My lip wobbled. I believed Weyland's explanation, but it didn't make the betrayal go away. "Were you really falling for me?" I needed to hear him say it again.

"No," Weyland said. "I *fell* in love with you. I am maddeningly, irrevocably in love with you, and I want to spend the rest of my life falling deeper. I know I fucked up, and if that means I have to follow you to Ethlow to make up for that, I will give up my ship and the sea." Weyland's hand was rough against my uninjured cheek, but he cradled my face with a deep gentleness that cracked my heart open.

The logical choice was to walk away from Weyland, but I was past logic.

I knelt next to my trunk and dug through the clothes shoved inside. The small jar Satella had gifted me sat on the bottom, untouched. As I unscrewed the lid, I approached the demon who had stolen my heart. With two fingers, I scooped some of the salve out. I carefully brushed it over the gaping wound on Weyland's chest. It was healing slowly, but if it wasn't dressed properly, it could lead to infection, even with the captain's enhanced healing.

The skin knitted together before my eyes. The salve was unlike anything I had seen.

"What is that?" Weyland's breath was shallow as he looked between the jar and his wound.

"Something the healer at Ethlow gave me. It's made from a rare flower."

"And you're willing to use it on me, Sunshine?" The familiarity of his nickname cracked my chest open.

My eyes met the captain's, and I knew I was screwed. "You see, I have this dilemma. I don't want to see you injured, because I, too, am maddeningly, irrevocably in love with you, which scares the shit out of me, because you have my heart. That means you can break it over and over again, and I would still be yours."

Weyland pressed his forehead against mine. "Good thing I have no intention of ever letting you get hurt again. You are my end game, Sunshine."

"I had better be." Tears broke free from the gates and streamed down my face.

Weyland wiped them away before kissing me deeply. All the pain I had felt before floated away, just as I would have if Weyland hadn't been holding onto me. Maybe it was stupid to give him my heart, but it was too late. It had belonged to him before we stepped onto Dragon's Breath Island, and I needed to believe that he would protect me, just as he had done since I stepped onto his ship.

Weyland kissed the top of my head as I leaned against the railing. I tucked my wings together to give him room to wrap his arms around my waist. I pressed into his warmth, letting it counter the bite of the winter winds.

"Where do you want to go first, Sunshine?" Weyland nipped my pointed ear, making me giggle.

"I get to choose?" I craned my neck to look back at the demon. His silver eye was sparkling, and his black eye looked lighter than usual.

"I told you I would follow you anywhere, and I meant it." He nuzzled his face into my neck, giving me goosebumps and dirty thoughts.

"First, we have to go back to Ethlow and give King Zathrian the Aethrium Stone." I touched the opal pendant around my neck, hoping it was what the king needed to save Ethlow.

"You could always keep it, and we could run away together."

I rolled my eyes, unsure if that was the response of a pirate or demon. It was definitely a pirate.

"That signet on your arm says otherwise." I traced the black mark of the demon king. The horns overlapped in the center, almost looking like a heart, which made me smile.

"We'll only be hunted by a demon king and the Shadow Slinger. I'm used to dodging powerful forces." Weyland's voice was light, but his grip on me tightened, making me question how dangerous going against King Zathrian would have been.

"That's not the first time you mentioned the Shadow Slinger and the king together." I had brushed off the comment last time, thinking it was a scare tactic for his crew, but there was no reason to use that on me.

"That's because he lives at Ethlow." Weyland shook his head. "How Zathrian got the ancient demon to work for him is a mystery I'll never understand."

"I've never seen him before." A shudder ran up my spine as I thought about the rumors I had heard about the Shadow Slinger. It was said that he was the most powerful demon in the underworld and mortal realm, and he could destroy entire villages with his shadows.

"You're joking."

"No?"

Weyland pulled back and turned me so we were facing each other. "The male you refer to as Master Viridian is the Shadow Slinger."

My instinct was to tell the pirate he was crazy, but as the information sank in, it made sense. Master Viridian used shadow magic—a rare form of power. Not only that, but the magic was older than I was by a significant amount. Those two things weren't enough to jump to the drastic solution, not when others like King Zathrian and Tareen, the librarian, also had magic older than me, but there were hundreds of little details that match the descriptions I had heard about the Shadow Slinger.

"That makes so much sense!" I gasped as all the pieces fell into place. "I thought he disappeared centuries ago."

"From the world, yes. He went to the one place someone can hide from the world and start over."

"Ethlow," I whispered. I didn't doubt Weyland was speaking the truth, but there were a hundred questions the news brought up. The most prevalent being, why would the Shadow Slinger move back to the shadows when he was rumored to be more powerful than the five demon rulers? What story had been hidden from the world to make the Shadow Slinger—to make Master Viridian—act as the right-hand male to the demon king?

"I was shocked when I found out, too."

"Shocked is an understatement. I'm flabbergasted." I shook my head, the information too much to process all at once.

Weyland's chuckle was enough for me to know he was laughing at my word choice. "I'm flabbergasted that you and others haven't figured it out after being there so long."

I pinched Weyland's side. "Sometimes the best place for someone to hide is in plain sight. Why would anyone suspect that the master of the house was really a powerful and terrifying demon that nearly destroyed the world?"

"I heard he saved it."

I rolled my eyes. "Either way, it's the same. And if you're right, there is no way I want you to break your deal with King Zathrian. Besides, there are things I want to do before we go on our grand adventures, friends I want to say goodbye to, things to pack. Oh, and I want to make sure the children are settled with a new teacher. I hate to leave them stranded."

"So, that'll take a few days?" Weyland asked.

"More like a few weeks." I didn't want to rush my leave at Ethlow, not when I already had a long list of tasks in my head.

"And then where to?" Weyland kissed my neck, making it difficult to think.

"I want to see Valenmae. The capital was built by fae, and it's absolutely gorgeous." I had always dreamed of visiting all five kingdoms in the mortal realm. I grew up in Lyranta, and Ethlow was part of Kinzlea—not that I had done much exploring—but with Weyland by my side, I knew I'd be able to see everything I had ever dreamed of. It was a strange and wonderful thought.

"Then we'll go to Valenmae, but right now, I think we should go to bed." Weyland nipped my ear, making my core burn. I wasn't about to argue with that.

I grabbed the pirate and flew towards his room, dragging him along behind me.

Chapter 28

It was strange to be back at Ethlow after months on the sea. The building appeared to be shrouded in darkness, something I hadn't noticed before. As I reached for the front door, I felt different, lighter. I had thought I had been happy at Ethlow, but it was clear I had simply been content.

The door swung open before I touched it, and I came face-to-face with Master Viridian—the Shadow Slinger. He tilted his head slowly. Small shadows danced along his shoulders and flickered in his eyes. After learning the truth, it seemed obvious.

"Miss Elcy, Miss Aukina, Reamann. Welcome home." Master Viridian bowed his head in greeting to us. Then he turned to Weyland. "I'm surprised you held up your end of the bargain."

Weyland chuckled. "Despite what you think of me, I don't break my word. Besides, this little thing served as a reminder of what was at stake." Weyland lifted his arm, but his leather coat blocked King Zathrian's signet.

"Wise decision." Master Viridian turned to Aukina and Reamann. "I expect you two to be back at work first thing tomorrow morning. Take the rest of the day to relax."

The couple nodded, and Aukina dragged Reamann inside as if she couldn't get away from the master of the house fast enough.

Master Viridian turned back to me. His eyes fell to my wings. "You're flying." It was a flat statement with no surprise. It was as if he noticed a haircut.

"They're working again." I couldn't help the smile that graced my lips.

"Zathrian is waiting for you in his office. Let's go." The demon turned on his heels, deciding the conversation was done. It wasn't uncommon behavior from the master of the house.

I squeezed Weyland's hand, nerves building in my stomach. I liked King Zathrian, but it made me nervous to be around authority figures, especially ones as powerful as the demon king and his second in command.

Master Viridian led us through the house. When we reached the stairs, I floated above them, making the trek up a breeze. When we reached King Zathrian's office, I wasn't winded like I had been before. The master of the house opened the door and let us walk in first. The king sat at his desk, but as soon as he saw us, his body perked up. His bright smile was the opposite of the tight-lipped demon next to me. Knowing who Master Viridian was only confused me more. The dynamic made no sense.

Master Viridian lifted a brow as he caught my eyes. His eyes flickered in recognition. The room grew chilly, and I had to fight against the shiver my body was on the verge of. I didn't know how, but Master Viridian knew I knew who he truly was.

"You look so tan, Elcy," King Zathrian said, breaking the gaze I was locked in with Master Viridian. "It looks good on you."

I cleared my throat and smiled at the compliment. "I've missed the sun." It wasn't impossible to enjoy the sun at Ethlow, but between teaching the children most of the day and dusk breaking earlier in the winter, it was hard to spend proper time outside.

"I understand that," the king said. His skin was always a deep tan, but I was sure his kingly duties kept him inside more often than not. His gaze shifted to the hand I had intertwined with Weyland's. When he looked back at me, his bright smile softened. "You're not staying, are you?"

The king's conclusion surprised me. I hadn't realized the decision was blatantly written on my face. "No, I'm going to return to the sea with Weyland, but I'm not leaving right away. I'd like a few weeks to get everything in order."

"You can have as much time as you need," King Zathrian said. "It's been an honor to have you as a resident, and you will be missed." I hardly knew the king, but I felt the sincerity of his words.

"Thank you. I appreciate everything you've provided for me when I had nothing." Tears pricked my eyes at the thought of leaving. Even if Ethlow hadn't been the life I wanted, it had been my home for twenty years. Leaving meant leaving a life I had built and friendships I had cultivated. I was excited about the next step in my adventure, but it wasn't easy to leave the familiarities I had grown to love.

Master Viridian cleared his throat. "As much as I love the sentimental moment occurring, there is a matter of the Aethrium Stone." His eyes narrowed on the necklace dangling between my breasts.

"Oh!" My eyes widened at the realization. I removed the necklace and set it on the desk in front of the king. My wings faltered without the power of the amulet, but after a moment, they recalibrated. I had kept the artifact close to me for so long that I felt empty without it. "Just as promised."

King Zathrian carefully took the amulet, his body tense as he inspected it. His yellow eyes glowed brighter the moment he touched the opal gem. He tightened his grip around it, and a slurry of emotions crossed his face. He put the necklace in his drawer and locked it.

"I hope you know what you have done for Ethlow and for Kinzlea, Elcy. Because of you, I can protect my kingdom. If you need anything at all on your future adventures, do not hesitate to reach out to me."

My chest warmed at the praise. "After everything you've done for me, I'm happy to return the favor."

The next several days were spent packing and organizing. I avoided telling everyone I was leaving as they welcomed me back home. I wasn't ready for the goodbyes that would follow with that information. I wanted to focus on the excitement of my next adventure before the melancholy of leaving set in.

Weyland laid on my bed, only a blanket covering his torso. "You don't have to do everything all at once. You should come back to bed, and you can do more tomorrow."

I licked my lips as I looked at the naked demon. It was like he had awoken an insatiable hunger inside of me. "I didn't think I could have this much stuff in a single room."

"Twenty years is a long time to collect shit. I say throw it all out, and we will get you new stuff." Weyland rolled to his side and propped his head with his hand. That position made the sheet stand up, pulling my attention to the demon's hard cock.

My breath hitched, and I knew I wouldn't be able to resist him for much longer. I climbed onto the bed with him, and he shifted us, so I was straddling him. The sheet and my bottoms separating our naked bodies were too much.

"I can't throw everything out. The things I have are memories I want to keep."

Weyland hooked his leg around mine and flipped us over. The sheet fell off him, leaving him completely exposed for me. He pressed himself against my core, his hardness creating friction between us. The chain tattoos came to life and wrapped around my wrists, pinning me to the bed.

"Let's make new memories, lots of ones filled with you moaning my name." He pressed his mouth against my neck and sucked on my skin.

"Weyland." His name unintentionally came out as a moan, but it was impossible to control myself with his tongue exploring my skin.

"Tell me what you want, Sunshine." He pulled at my shirt, giving him access to my collarbones. He nipped and sucked the sensitive skin.

"I want you to fuck me." I stretched my neck back, needing his tongue everywhere.

Weyland extended a black claw and used it to rip my shirt. I'd have to scold him for destroying my clothes later, but as his mouth found my nipple, I couldn't bring myself to complain. As he pulled away to give attention to the other breast, he said, "Tell me how you want me to fuck you."

His hands moved lower, his fingers hooking around the hem of my pants. Then he paused, waiting for me to answer him.

"I want you to fuck every hole and take full advantage of me."

Weyland let go of my pants and crawled back to my face. He grabbed my chin firmly. "Every hole?" He kissed me, slipping his tongue into my mouth. When he pulled back, he had a dangerous look in his eyes.

As the realization of what he meant washed over me, my eyes widened. I hesitated, but the thought of having him in my mouth excited me. "Yes," I breathed.

"I was hoping you'd say that." He kissed me again before pulling me to my knees on the bed.

He stood, making it so I was making eye contact with his cock. He stroked my hair before gently guiding me forward. I parted my lips and took the tip of him into my mouth. I flicked my tongue over the end, earning a deep groan. My core throbbed with excitement, and I wanted to make him feel good. I took more of him in my mouth, and he kept his hand on my head, gently stroking my hair and making me feel loved, even as I had him in my mouth.

I slowly picked up the pace, getting more confident about what made his body tense with pleasure.

"Fuck, Elcy. I love the way your pretty little mouth feels around me." Weyland stretched his neck back and thrusted to meet my mouth. He hit the back of my throat, making me gag. He pulled out quickly, but the separation didn't last long. He kissed me deeply before lifting me up. My legs wrapped around his torso, and my wings kept me propped up.

He adjusted himself at my pussy and slammed into me. I dug my nails into the back of his neck. He moved me up and down, and the position caused friction against my clit. It wasn't long before the sensations became too much, and I was coming on his cock. My head fell against his shoulder as he fucked me through my orgasm.

"You feel so fucking good around my cock." Weyland slammed me down harder, making my entire body shake.

A groan erupted from the demon's mouth. Weyland was close to his own finish. He pulled me off him and flipped me around. Chains wrapped around my wrists and pulled me forward, forcing me to bend over for him. He pushed his fingers into my ass, making sure I was ready for him before he pushed inside. He picked up his pace and intensity from before, making my body feel alive.

For a century, I didn't know it was possible for anyone to make me feel so damned good, especially not a male. Others only cared about getting themselves off, but not Weyland. He always made sure I found my pleasure at least once before he found his own, and after, he took care of me. There were moments it didn't feel real, like it was a dream that would slip through my fingers one day. Even if that was the case, I planned on enjoying every moment I had with the pirate captain.

"Weyland," I moaned, feeling the pressure build again.

The chains pulled me upright, and Weyland grabbed my neck, guiding my face to his. "Come for me, Sunshine." He kissed me while snaking his hand to my clit and stroking it until the pleasure exploded inside of me.

He slammed into me one last time before filling me with his own pleasure. He held me close, kissing me softly as we both came down from our highs.

"We should get you cleaned up and dressed in something pretty." Weyland picked me up and brought me to the washroom connected to my room. It was small compared to the community bath, but it worked for basic purposes.

"Something pretty?" I asked. He had never mentioned my style of clothes before.

"I have a surprise for you."

Chapter 29

Weyland held my hand, leading me through the estate with surprising familiarity.

"Where are we going?" I asked.

Weyland wore a pair of tight leather pants that showed off his firm ass. He wore a silk red shirt that hung loosely around his torso. The shirt was tucked into his pants, emphasizing the V-shape of his torso. Despite everything we had done, I craved his touch.

"Right back to the bedroom if you don't control your thoughts." He squeezed my hand, and his eyes flashed with desire.

I licked my lips, swallowing hard. Would the never-ending need ever stop? "I wouldn't be opposed."

A low growl rumbled through his chest. "Nyri will kill me if we're any later than we are."

I furrowed my brows. "What does Nyri have to do with any of this?"

Weyland pulled me into the grand hall, and a chorus of surprises erupted around us, making me take a step back. Everyone I knew had gathered in the large room, dressed in their best clothes, and it was decorated with flowers and orbs of magic. I looked at Weyland for an explanation.

"A certain vampire mentioned it's your century birthday today," Weyland said. "You may be young, but this is an important birthday to celebrate."

I hadn't told many about my birthday, but Satella must have remembered. I hadn't said anything to Weyland, since there was too much going on, and I didn't want to bother him, but he had found out, anyway.

Nyri skipped up to me and took my hands. King Zathrian was a step behind her. "Happy birthday, Elcy! Sorry for the last minute party, but I didn't know it was your birthday, otherwise the party would have been better. I talked to Zath, and he said throwing a party was a great idea and the perfect way to say goodbye."

Tears pricked at my eyes. The party was more than I had ever expected. "You did all of this for me?"

"You risked your life for us. It's the least we can do," King Zathrian said. He wrapped his arm around Nyri's waist and pulled her close to him.

"And there's a lot of people who want to celebrate you and say goodbye." Nyri beamed proudly. She cared about the residents of Ethlow, which made her a suitable partner for the demon king. I only hoped it didn't put her in too much danger.

"This is incredible." I wiped my eyes before tears could fall. I wasn't ready to say goodbye to anyone. There was still time before we left.

Nyri grabbed my hand, as if sensing that. "Tonight is about having fun and enjoying our time together while we can. Tears are for another day, so let's dance and forget the rest."

Music filled the room as Nyri dragged me to the dance floor where the rest of her friends were waiting. Satella hugged me, wishing me a happy birthday. Tareen smiled and waved, saying she was glad I made it back safely. Aukina immediately went into telling the others how brave I was on Dragon's Breath Island, making my cheeks flush.

For a moment, I saw what kind of life I'd have if I stayed at Ethlow, but when I looked back at Weyland, who was watching me from the sidelines, I couldn't stop the smile that took over. I told myself I'd see my friends at Ethlow again, but it was time I started living for myself.

The party continued on well into the night, and when it started dwindling down, Weyland pulled me to the dance floor. His hands rested on my hips as we swayed back and forth.

"Are you sure you want to spend the rest of your life on the seas with a cranky bastard like me when you have so many people who care about you here?" His fingers dug into my back, as if he was afraid of my answer.

"I love the beings who live at Ethlow," I said, "but I think I love you more. You made me remember what it felt like to be free, and I'm done with putting my life on hold out of fear." My wings fluttered, making pixie dust fill the air. Weyland spun us around, and with the glowing dust blocking out the rest of the dance floor, it felt like it was him and me against the world.

"Good." He kissed me deeply, not caring who saw us. "Because I could use more sunshine in my life, and I can't imagine what life would look like without you."

"You'd be using your hand a lot more." I bit my lip and looked away from the demon, knowing that comment would come back to haunt me later.

Weyland pinched my ass, making me squeak. "Maybe I should make you use your hand while I watch." His voice was low in my ear, making my body shiver.

"You wouldn't." My eyes widened, embarrassed by the thought of touching myself in front of him.

"Let's test that theory." Weyland nipped my lip before grabbing my hand, ready to pull me back to the bedroom.

"I should say goodbye first," I said, looking back at the party, but my eyes landed on the balcony looking over the estate.

Staring at me between the railings was a rat with one red eye and one yellow. My heart pounded at the sight of the shapeshifter. I kept her secret, because I had felt like I owed it to her. If she was at Ethlow, I needed to warn someone, especially if she was after the Aethrium Stone.

In the blink of an eye, Kestria shifted into a person, posing with her finger to her mouth. She winked at me before she shifted again, back to the rat. I looked to see if anyone noticed, but everyone had been too absorbed in the party.

"What are you looking at?" Weyland pulled me against his torso, his mouth finding my neck. The sensations made my worries float away.

Kestria was a good person. I didn't know her well, but that was what my gut feeling was telling me. "Nothing." I glanced back up to the balcony, but Kestria was gone. Shadows danced along the area she had been a moment prior, as if they were chasing her essence.

"Then let's hurry, because I have plans for you." Weyland kissed me and pulled me along to my room. I wasn't going to worry about Kestria, not when she saved me. She wouldn't have done that if she only intended to hurt anyone else. Her presence was something to worry about another day. It was my birthday, and I was going to spend the rest of it with the dreaded pirate, Captain Weyland—the demon who stole my heart.

AUTHOR'S NOTE

Thank you so much for taking time to read my book! If you've made it this far, I would greatly appreciate it if you took the time to leave a review on Amazon/Goodreads. As an indie author, reviews are essential for gaining more visibility. All reviews are appreciated! If you ever have any questions, concerns, or general comments, please feel free to reach out to me directly at evereri.theauthor@gmail.com!

Also by EverEri

Read more in The Demons of Kinzlea

The Demon King's Pet
The Demon King's Cook
The Demon King's Healer
The Demon King's Librarian
The Demon King's Teacher
The Demon King's Assassin

Coming Soon!

The Demon Queen's Rise
Coming in early 2025

The Unfortunate Fate of Mates

Available on the Dreame App:

The Four Beta Brothers
The Stolen Wolf Princess
The Long Lost Luna
The Unwanted Wolf
The Blood Moon Twins

ACKNOWLEDGEMENTS

I am continuously shocked by the amount of support I receive from my friends and family. Thank you for listening to me when I am struggling on this difficult path I have chosen, and thank you for letting me celebrate the wins that make this journey worth it. Thank you for reading my books and giving me new ideas for more. This book series has grown into something bigger than I ever expected, and I am grateful to everyone who has made that possible.

A special thanks to Lauren for inspiring the character of Elcy. Your passion for this book series only makes me want to do so much more.

A thank you to Kelly. Without you, this book would have fallen flat, and all of your feed back was essential for this.

A thank you to Paula for getting just as excited about numbers and calculations as me, and supporting this career path, even when things feel impossible.

ABOUT THE AUTHOR

 EverEri is a lover of romance, fantasy, and fairytales, and one of her favorite things to do is to bring a story and characters alive through the written word. EverEri began her true writing journey in the paranormal romance world in 2021, and she never plans to turn back. Whether it's demons, dragons, werewolves, merfolk, or other magical beings, she plans to bring her passions to life in each book she writes.

Want to see more?

Follow EverEri on social media:

IG: everlastingeri

Tik Tok: author_evereri

FB: EverEri's Reading Group

Newsletter: evereri.theauthor@gmail.com

www.ingramcontent.com/pod-product-compliance
Lightning Source LLC
Chambersburg PA
CBHW050039180626
46810CB00002B/801